Magical Children

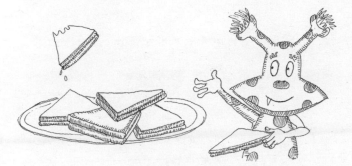

Sally Gardner had a very successful career as a
designer of sets and costumes for the theatre before
she turned to writing and illustrating books for children,
which was what she always wanted to do. Her books
are extremely popular and include *Fairy Shopping*,
The Glass Heart, *The Fairy Catalogue*, and *A Book of
Princesses*, as well as the Magical Children series. She is
now writing her first full-length novel for older readers,
I, Coriander. She has a teenage son and grown-up
twin daughters and lives in London.

Magical Children

3 books in 1

The Strongest Girl in the World

The Invisible Boy

The Boy Who Could Fly

Sally Gardner

Dolphin Paperbacks

This collection first published in Great Britain in 2004
by Dolphin Paperbacks
an imprint of Orion Children's Books
a division of the Orion Publishing Group Ltd
5 Upper Saint Martin's Lane
London WC2H 9EA

A catalogue record for this book is available
from the British Library.

Printed and bound in Great Britain by
Clays Ltd, St Ives plc

ISBN 1 84255 104 3

www.orionbooks.co.uk

Contents

The Strongest
Girl in the World

To Diani Bell for
all her love and friendship

1

Josie could do many tricks. She could balance a pencil on the end of her finger. She could pick her nose without anyone seeing. She could tickle the cat until it said Stop it! But her best trick happened at ten-thirty one Friday morning. It was a trick that changed her life.

It happened in the school playground when Billy Brand got his head stuck in the school railings. His teacher, Mrs Jones, came to help. It was no good. Billy Brand's head would not budge. The school nurse came to have a look. Billy Brand was going very red. The headmaster, Mr Murray, called the fire brigade. The dinner lady put butter on Billy Brand's swollen face but still he could not squeeze his head through the railings. Billy Brand was well and truly stuck.

All the children crowded round to have a look. This was the best fun they had had all week.

"Will he explode, miss?" asked a little lad.

"Miss, miss, will they have to cut off his head?" asked another.

"No," said Mrs Jones. "Now, children, please don't all crowd round."

Billy Brand started to cry.

It was then that Josie Jenkins, aged eight and nine months, knew that she could do her trick. She felt a whizz of power down her arm into her fingers.

She went over to the iron railings and bent them right back. It was like pulling tissue paper apart, easy-peasy. Billy Brand's head was no longer stuck. There was a stunned silence, then a loud cheer. Mrs Jones couldn't believe her eyes. There stood Billy Brand, a little red in the face, with butter on his ears, but free.

At that moment Mr Murray came running into the playground, followed by the fire brigade. All the children were now trying to see if they could bend the school railings, which they couldn't. Billy Brand was standing in the middle of them looking rather red and silly.

"What is the meaning of this?" said Mr Murray, looking at Billy Brand. "How did you get free? Mrs Jones, what is going on here?"

Mrs Jones, who was quite lost for words, pointed at Josie. "Well," said Mr Murray, "is this some kind of trick?"

"Yes, sir," said Josie. "I could see Billy was stuck so I just unstuck him."

The fire officer was looking at the bent school railing. "Who did this?" he asked.

"I did, sir," said Josie.

Mr Murray looked as if he might explode at any minute.

"Josie," he said, "those railings are made out of iron. No one can bend iron, especially not an eight-year-old girl. That is why I called the fire brigade."

"Shall I straighten them out again, sir?" asked Josie.

"Don't talk such drivel!" said Mr Murray.

Josie walked over to the railings and in front of the whole school, in front of the fire officer, she gently put the railings back as they were.

That evening Josie was having tea with her
family, Mum, Dad and big brother Louis. She
hadn't told anyone about what had
happened at school. She had a small feeling
that no one would believe her. Even Mrs
Jones, her teacher, had told the whole class
that it was just a trick that Billy Brand and
Josie had thought up between them. Billy
Brand had had to stand all afternoon
outside Mr Murray's door. Josie had had to

write a hundred times I won't do any more tricks.

"You're very quiet, my love," said Dad. "Everything all right?"

"Yes," Josie mumbled. She thought there was a chance her dad might understand about the school railing. He often told her that magic is all around us except people don't want to see it. But as for Louis who was twelve and clever, best to keep quiet.

After tea and telly, Josie went to her bedroom. She just had to see if she could still do her trick. She picked up her bedroom chair. It was as light as a pencil. She was just balancing it at the end of her finger when Louis walked into her bedroom. Usually Josie hated Louis barging into her bedroom. But not tonight.

"Josie, what are you doing?" he laughed. "Trying to be the strongest girl in the world? Come on, put the chair down before you hurt yourself." Josie put the chair down gracefully and with no trouble at all.

9

"You do it, Louis," she said.

"Oh, give us a break. Pick up a chair! That is so easy, it's sad! But if it makes you happy..."

Louis picked up the chair. It was much heavier than he thought. There was no way he could balance it on one finger. Then he nearly dropped it. Finally he banged it down heavily on the floor. He was not going to let his baby sister show him up. He went over to Josie and patted her on the head. "That's a good girl. Time for bed."

For once Josie was not cross with Louis. She knew her trick hadn't gone away.

The next morning Josie was up and downstairs before Louis. Her dad was eating his breakfast. "Well Josie, my love, off to watch the cartoons?"

"No Dad," said Josie. "I want to help you at work today."

Josie loved where her dad worked. He owned a small garage where he mended old cars. She would always take him his lunch on a Saturday and he would push his tools off the bench so that his little princess could sit next to him and not get dirty. But she had never before gone to work with him. That was Louis' job.

"All right," said Dad, "you can answer the phone and make us coffee." It was not quite what Josie had in mind but it would have to do. She waited all morning until her chance came.

"I'm just popping out for a minute with

Louis. Answer the phone if it rings and don't touch anything."

Josie went over to the car her dad had been working on. This was what she had been waiting for. Would her trick work on cars as it had on the school railings and on her chair? She put her tiny arm out and held on to the bumper of the car. Then she lifted. Yes! Yes! she could do it. The car was no heavier than her school rucksack. With a bit of careful handling she could balance it on the palm of her hand.

That was how Dad and Louis found her: this skinny little girl in a dress holding up a Ford Cortina.

"Don't move!" screamed Dad. "Louis, call 999 and get the fire brigade fast."

Josie carefully put the car down. "Don't call them," she said. "They don't like my tricks."

12

The rest of the day Dad and Louis tested Josie's so-called trick. There was no doubt about it. This little girl was amazingly strong.

"You're all very quiet tonight," said Mum as they ate their tea. "Cat got your tongues?"

Dad cleared his throat. "Joan," he said, "there is something we have got to tell you."

"Oh Josie," said Mum. "You didn't fiddle with anything in the garage?"

"No," said Dad, "nothing like that. It's just - well - Josie is probably the strongest little girl in the world."

Her mum burst out laughing until tears rolled down her face.

"Oh, Ron, you say some daft things."

Dad gave Josie a wink and she lifted the tea table up as though it were a book and swirled it around on her finger. Mum sat back in her chair, as white as a newly washed sheet.

"That's nothing," said Louis with pride. "My

little sister can lift a car that would need a crane and..."

"Hold on a minute," said Mum. "Are you telling me that our little girl, who is small for her age, and skinny to boot, who looks as if a gust of wind could blow her away, can lift a car?"

"Yes," said Josie. Then she told her mum about the school railings.

"Well, what do we do?" said Mum. "I mean,

who would believe it?"

"We do and say *nothing*," said Dad. "We keep it to ourselves for the time being."

"You don't think she should see a doctor?" said Mum.

"Oh, Mum," said Louis. "Josie's fine. She's just amazingly strong."

"Well, Josie," said Mum, "you're still my little girl, strong or not." And she gave her a big hug.

Josie was not looking forward to Monday morning. In class assembly, Mr Murray, the head teacher, gave a talk on the wrongs of showing off, and playing silly tricks in the playground. Even her teacher, Mrs Jones, still seemed to be cross with her. Worst of all, she was now the butt of all the jokes.

"How does it feel to be a hairy strong girl?"

"Hey, here comes Superman's sidekick."

It went on like this all day. Only Billy Brand stood up for her.

"That's it," thought Josie. "Dad's right." Best to keep this trick to herself.

Never had Josie been more pleased to hear the home bell ring. There was her mum waiting for her.

"Ready for tea, love?" said Mum.

"Not half," said Josie. "It's been a really bad day." They walked out of the school playground towards the main road. That's when it happened. That's when nothing would quite be the same again.

A van came charging out of control down the hill towards the zebra crossing, towards Josie and her mum and all her chums. The driver was running behind it, shouting as loud as he could. Nothing was going to stop it. Josie had that whizzing feeling in her arms and without another thought she ran into the road, putting her skinny arm at the

ready to stop the van. It was no heavier
than catching a football and a lot easier on
account of its size. The van stopped in its
tracks, no damage done. There was a
moment of stunned silence while the crowd
took in what had happened. Then chaos.
Mums and dads fainted. The lollipop lady
went dizzy and the owner of the van
couldn't believe what he had seen.

When the police and the
ambulance arrived,

they thought there must have been an
awful accident; there were bodies lying all
over the place. The lollipop lady was
mumbling something about a little girl. The
van driver was sitting on the pavement
saying it must be magic. The poor
policeman in charge didn't know what to
think. And there standing in the middle of
the road was a little girl holding on to a van.

"Are you all right?" said the policeman.

"Oh, fine," said Josie, "but I can't let go
because it could start to roll again."

They're all mad, thought the policeman. He
said, "It would be a good idea if you got out
of the road and left that van alone."

Josie did as she was told.

"Now," said the policeman, taking a notepad from his jacket. "Can anyone tell me what happened?"

But before the policeman could write a line, the van started to roll away again.

Josie ran back into the road and stopped it for the second time.

"Thank you," said the policeman. "Now, where was I?"

It took quite a lot of clear thinking on Mum's part to stop the policeman from taking Josie down to the police station for further questioning.

6

At home Dad was pacing up and down the living room carpet.

"I am sorry," said Josie. "I just did it without thinking."

Her dad looked up. "Poppet, you did the right thing. You are a very brave and strong little girl."

"Nothing will happen, will it?" said Josie, looking at her dad's worried face.

"No, it's just that the paper will get hold of the story and I don't know what they will make of it."

The doorbell rang. "Hello, Mrs Jenkins," came a soft-spoken voice. "My name is Avril Ghoast and I'm from the local paper, the *Echo*. I wonder if I could have a word with you about your daughter?"

Josie stood in the living room with Mum and Dad, looking small and worried in a pretty dress and shiny shoes. Avril Ghoast was sure that this was all a huge joke. No one would believe that this will-of-the-wisp could stop a bike, let alone a van.

"It's a joke, isn't it?" said Avril, looking at Mum and Dad. "Sorry to waste your time. This is my first job as a reporter and I suppose the lads at work thought it would be a bit of a laugh to send me here."

"Well then, the laugh's on them," said Dad.

"Ron, no," said Mum, "I don't think we should say anything."

"It's no good, Joan," said Dad. "It's out now.

The best we can do is let Avril know the true story, not some made-up nonsense."

That is how Avril Ghoast made her first huge break as a journalist. A photographer from the *Echo* came to photograph Josie lifting the Ford Cortina. It was headlined in the local paper. It was headlined in the national papers too.

The next day a TV crew turned up to film Josie. The TV reporter wore trendy glasses.

"We need to see this on film," he kept saying. "I mean, how do we know that this is not a trick?"

"It *is* a trick," said Josie. "It's my best ever trick."

The TV reporter gave a nervous laugh. He turned to Dad and said, "I have just got back from India where I was supposed to film an elephant lifting a car. When I got there, the elephant wouldn't or couldn't do it. I was left with the whole village saying they saw the elephant lift the car on Tuesday or was it a truck on Wednesday. I came home with nothing. I bet," he added, looking glumly at Josie, "this is just another White Elephant story."

"Can I change before I lift the car again?" said Josie.

"Do what you like," said the TV reporter, fiddling with his glasses. "I'm sure it won't make the slightest difference."

"Well then," said Dad, "I think you will be in for a bit of a shock."

Josie put on her prettiest party dress, brushed her hair and put on one of Mum's old hats. When the TV reporter saw her, he didn't know whether to laugh or cry.

"I'm a bit fed up with lifting the same old car.

If it's all the same to you, could I see if I can lift a bus?"

"A bus," repeated the reporter. "Why not! Let's do a bus."

They all trooped down to the local bus station. "Which do you fancy?" said the TV reporter, looking at his watch. "I haven't got all day."

Josie went over to an empty double decker bus. This would be the biggest test of her trick yet. She went round to the front and lifted it up on to her shoulder without any trouble. It weighed no more than an empty rucksack. Josie pushed the bus up until she was balancing it on the palms of her hands.

"This is wonderful! Oh my word!" shouted the TV reporter, who seemed suddenly to have come to life. "I am standing in the bus station with Josie Jenkins who is eight years old and probably the strongest little girl in Britain, in the world, in the universe..."

Josie liked this. She took one hand off the

bus and straightened her hat. She wanted to look her best. She had never been on television before. The main news story that night was about Josie Jenkins' incredible strength.

7

Stanley Arnold, the strongest man in Britain, was watching the news that night. He didn't find the story about Josie Jenkins very funny. Who was this little girl who had the cheek to go about lifting up cars and buses, that's what he wanted to know. He called his agent. "What is all this nonsense about Josie Jenkins?"

A few squeaks could be heard down the phone.

"I don't care what you say. I want to show everybody that this little upstart is having us all on." A few more squeaks came out of the end of the phone. "No one, I repeat no one, is stronger than Stanley Arnold. I want a competition. That will show her up for the fraud she is."

No one argued with Stanley Arnold. He ate beef wholesale.

"You don't have to do this silly competition, poppet," said Dad. But Josie was cross. "How dare he say that I'm having everyone on!" she said.

"I'll kill him," said Louis. "He has no right to be so rude about my little sister."

"Now," said Mum. "Shall we all just calm down. Josie doesn't have to go in for any competition. She doesn't have to prove anything to anybody."

"Especially not to Stanley Arnold," muttered Dad.

But Josie liked the idea of a competition. It gave her a good tingling feeling just to think about it.

Stanley Arnold went in for serious body building. Josie went shopping and bought some very pretty shoes that she had been wanting for ages.

The day arrived. It was held in a football stadium so that the crowds could get in. Stanley Arnold arrived with his agent, his personal trainer, his publicity lady and his fan club. Josie arrived with Mum, Dad and Louis.

"Well, on looks alone, we know who's won," laughed Dad. "Now Josie, don't go hurting yourself. Stop at any time."

The competition was divided into three parts. First part: dragging a car for three metres. Second part: throwing a barrel over a wall. Third part: a tug of war.

Stanley Arnold went first. He dragged his
car, going red in the face, every muscle in
his body ready to pop. But he got the car
across the finishing line. The crowd roared.
A commentator said it was Stanley Arnold's
fastest time.

Now it was Josie's turn. She walked over
to the car, sucking a lollipop. She had lifted
them up lots of times but she had never
walked with a car. The huge crowd went
quiet. Josie lifted the front of the car and

balanced it on one hand, like a waiter
holding a tray. She walked past Stanley's car
to the other side of the football pitch, still
sucking her lollipop. The crowd went wild.
Stanley Arnold looked even wilder. The
commentator said Josie Jenkins had broken
all known records.

Next was throwing the barrel over the
wall. This is what Stanley Arnold did best. In
fact he was famous for throwing the barrel.

He took a long run, then, with a grunt, let go. The barrel went high into the air and landed with a loud bang behind the wall. The crowd went crazy. The commentator went crazy. "This is a world record for barrel throwing."

Then it was Josie's go. She picked up the barrel and threw it as if it was a tennis ball. The barrel whizzed higher and higher up into the air, so high that it could not be seen. Then, like a rocket, it hit the ground,

making a huge crater. The crowd was silent.
The commentator said in a quiet voice of
disbelief, "Josie Jenkins has broken all
known world records for barrel throwing."

The Grand Finale was the tug of war. Stanley
Arnold had been sprayed down. He flexed
his muscles and chalk was put into his hand.
For extra grip, Josie pulled up her socks.

The rope was very thick. Josie took one
end and before she was ready, Stanley gave
a mighty pull. Josie landed in the dirt and
grazed her knee. The crowd booed.

The referee walked on to the
pitch. Josie pulled herself up.
She thought Stanley Arnold
was very rude.

"On the count of three,
pull..." yelled the referee.

One, two, three. Josie
grabbed hold of the rope.
The whizz in her arms was
so powerful that it was like

pulling the string on a kite. Stanley
Arnold, the strongest man in
Britain, felt his feet leave the
ground as he spun
round and round the
football pitch. It
was a sensational
victory. There
could be no
doubt that this was the
strongest girl in Britain.

Stanley Arnold got into his large car and
went home, saying it was an insult to his
strength to perform with a human freak.

8

Josie hadn't changed one little bit. But her life had. Before her trick there had been time to play with her friends, to watch videos with Louis. Now hardly a day went by without someone wanting Josie to show off her incredible strength.

It had been good fun at first. Her teacher, Mrs Jones, had said she was sorry for not believing Josie, and so had the headmaster. None of the children teased her. In fact, she was quite a star; a star to everyone in fact except the person she really wanted to impress - Louis. Why couldn't he see this was her greatest trick ever? Instead, he was constantly putting her down. "Not much skill in lifting cars," he would say, or "You'll end up with muscles like Popeye's."

Louis didn't like Josie's trick one little bit. He was fed up with everyone talking about his baby sister. In truth, Louis was jealous, green with the stuff. Heck, he used to be the strong one. He used to be responsible for his little sister. How could he look after the strongest girl in the world? Only Superman's older brother would know how Louis was feeling. That's if Superman *had* an older brother, which he didn't.

Then came an offer that would change all their lives. Mr Two Suit flew in from New York just to see the girl with the mighty strength.

The Jenkinses had

never met anyone quite like Mr Two Suit before. He had a face like a potato and a fake flower where his heart should have been.

"The offer," he said, smiling his most charming smile so that his two gold teeth shone, "is this. I take you and your family to New York to do some serious shopping!"

It sounded like a fairy tale. Mr Two Suit pulled a fat envelope from his front pocket. "Fame and fortune will be yours, Mr and Mrs Jenkins. Just sign the contract here, if you please."

Dad signed. How he could he refuse? They'd never been further than Blackpool.

9

New York was amazing, with buildings so tall they could talk to the stars.

41

"This is well wicked," said Louis. They were staying in the Plaza Hotel in their very own suite.

"There are more rooms here than we have at home," said Mum.

There were flowers everywhere. A bath the size of a swimming pool. Room service on tap.

"This is the life," said Dad.

Sam Two Suit had got Josie a publicity
lady, a clothes designer, a hairdresser, a
manicurist, a personal trainer and a
chauffeur with a stretch limo to take them
wherever they wanted to go.

Josie was transformed, with puffed-up hair
and a frilly shiny dress. Mum and Dad
looked barely recognizable. Louis looked just
about all right.

"What have they done to you, Josie? You look like a living doll," said Louis.

Josie agreed but she wasn't going to let on to Louis. "I think I look pretty," she said.

"Yes, pretty awful," said Louis.

"That's enough of that," said Mr Two Suit, "I love it, the camera will love it, and the public will love it. Just think of the Look Alike Dolls we'll be able to sell."

But Josie didn't feel right. She didn't feel like Josie Jenkins.

The next morning Josie was photographed lifting up a car outside the Plaza. The picture appeared on the front page of several newspapers. The headline read: *Josie Jenkins age 8 challenges America to find someone stronger!*

10

As it happened there was no shortage of people willing to pit their strength and their money against Josie Jenkins.

The first of many challenges took place on a beach on Long Island. Josie was dressed in a designer swimsuit and was wearing a hat. She was to beat the record for carrying cement-filled barrels from a raft in the bay back to the shore. Mum didn't like the look of this at all.

"She could drown, Ron," she wailed, "lifting those barrels."

"Joan," said Dad, "for goodness sake! Josie is going to be fine. What is a cement-filled barrel compared to a car?"

There was one small problem. The raft had been put too far out in the sea. Josie couldn't stand up. However, this was put right and Josie managed to arrange her cement barrels in neat building blocks

which needed a crane to take them down.

"Things are going great," said Sam Two
Suit. "Tomorrow you've a date to pull a
truck, princess. That'll wow them!"

Josie wasn't listening. She was longing to

go swimming with Louis.

"Last one into the sea is a green banana!" she shouted, about to run into the waves.

"Hold it right there, princess," said Mr Two Suit. "The strongest little girl in the world doesn't play. She trains. That's why I have provided you with a gym and a personal trainer."

Of course, Josie had never used a gym or a personal trainer. It wasn't *that* sort of a trick.

11

It wasn't long before Mr Big Country
himself took up the challenge. He bet more
dollars than sense that Josie couldn't lift his
horse off the ground.

Quite a crowd turned up on the day, plus
a TV crew. This was a story worth filming.
Mr Big Country was big. His horse was big.
Josie was small, very small indeed.
Mr Two Suit rubbed his chubby
hands together.

"It'll make a great picture,"
he said.

"But next time, I want her in a designer dress."

"It's not the dress that matters," said Mum anxiously. "It's that horse."

"Quit the whining, Mrs Jenkins, and smile. You're on camera," said Mr Two Suit, grinning.

Mum couldn't smile. She was far too worried. "She could get badly hurt," she said.

Mr Two Suit wasn't interested. He was looking at the future. His future paved with gold, with Josie making him the richest man in the world.

The horse turned out to be a calm and well-behaved animal who longed for his owner, Mr Big Country, to sweep him off his hooves high into the air.

Mr Big Country puffed himself up like a turkey, then lifted his horse a few centimetres off the ground. The crowd clapped politely, the horse looked disappointed and Mr Big Country gave a satisfied smirk. He was famous for lifting up his horse.

"Beat that, little girl, if you can," he said.

Josie wasn't sure. Her dad tried to sound upbeat. "You can do it, poppet," he urged, though to tell the truth he could see how Josie might feel that her trick wasn't up to lifting a live animal.

Suddenly Mr Two Suit's vision of the future became horribly clear. He could see himself losing a lot of money. He wasn't about to allow this to happen. No two bit horse was going to stand in his way to fame and fortune.

"Lift that horse, Josie Jenkins," yelled Mr Two Suit. "I order you to lift that horse."

"This is crazy," said Mr Big Country. "That skinny kid couldn't lift a candy bar. I think you owe me one mighty big cheque!"

It was at this moment that the horse whispered something into Josie's ear. Then, to everyone's amazement, she lifted the horse by his hind legs as high as she could, which was a lot higher than Mr Big Country had managed.

The horse snorted. He had waited his whole life for this moment. He reared into the air with Josie holding on tightly and stayed there for what seemed like forever. The crowd went crazy. The film crew couldn't get enough of it. Finally, with a smile, Josie put the horse gently down.

Mr Big Country looked rather small as he handed over his money to Mr Two Suit. The horse on the other hand was one happy animal. This was something to boast about to his friends in the stable.

12

It soon became clear that Josie Jenkins and her family were nothing more than a circus act and Mr Two Suit the greedy ringmaster. Every day there was a new city, a new challenge. It all flashed by so fast that soon the challenges merged together in one large blur.

At first Dad had loved all the razzamatazz that surrounded Josie. He felt like a star trainer as he urged Josie on to yet more incredible feats of strength, but pretty soon he, like Mum, became worried that Josie really would hurt herself. Josie's parents began to think that it had all got out of hand

and should be stopped. Louis agreed. He longed to get back and see his friends and his home again. He didn't like having to live in the goldfish bowl of publicity. As for Josie, the star of it all, what she wanted was to do something useful rather than these endless challenges that helped no one. Superman saved people, didn't he? The world, the universe, that sort of thing. He hadn't ended up as part of a circus act. If this was all she could do, she would rather go home.

"How is it that such a great trick can go so wrong?" she asked Louis gloomily. They were in their hotel room listening to Mum and Dad arguing next door.

Mum was saying, "Enough is enough, Ron."
Then more muffled words from Dad.

"And what about the garage?" said Mum.
"You'll lose all your customers if they find
that their cars haven't been mended."

"I know," shouted Dad. "But what can we
do?"

What they did was tell Mr Two Suit they
were going home.

13

"Home!" said Mr Two Suit, rolling the sound in his mouth like a gobstopper. "Home," he repeated slowly as if waiting for it to change colour. He glowered at Josie. "You can't," he said flatly. "I own you, the lot of you. I own Josie Jenkins Incorporated. You," he said, pointing at Dad, "signed the contract. If you break it, Mr Jenkins, I'll sue you for every penny you have. Do you understand?"

They understood all right. They were well and truly caught in Mr Two Suit's net. In no time at all, he had Mum and Dad bundled off to Florida to a Home for Irritating and Worrisome Parents. They didn't even get the chance to say goodbye. Louis was allowed to stay with Josie as long as he was good.

So here they were, stuck on the twelfth floor of the Plaza Hotel, Louis and Josie by themselves and with no way of getting home.

Josie looked miserable and Louis gave
her a hug.

"Don't worry," he said. " We're in this
together, And somehow we are going to
get out together."

14

Louis had a plan. It was quite simple. At the first opportunity that came along, Josie would talk to the TV reporters and tell them what had happened, and how they wanted their mum and dad back so that they could go home.

The next day Mr Two Suit came in. He was very excited.

"I have a major deal! A breakfast cereal company wants you to star in their commercial. All you have to do is lift this three storey house, lock, stock and barrel, and move it to a new site."

"Why?" said Louis. "That sounds daft."

"Look, wise guy, I am getting pretty sick of you," said Mr Two Suit. "If you can't put a sock in it, I'll send you away too."

"No!" shrieked Josie.

"Sorry," said Louis.

Mr Two Suit turned to Josie. "Filming being

today, I want you to look your prettiest, princess. After all this is the big time – Hollywood!"

Lifting the house wasn't going to be easy. It wasn't the fact that it was three storeys high. After all, she seemed to be getting stronger by the day. And it wasn't the weight that bothered Josie. It was the tunnel they had dug beneath it so that Josie could crawl in to lift the house from its foundations.

Josie was scared of spiders

and she was worried about all the crawly insects that would appear, like when you lift up a stone. Mr Two Suit couldn't care less.

"For heaven's sake, what's your problem? How can a few insects frighten the strongest girl in the world? Give me a break!"

"We would like to get started," said the lady director, "so can we have some action."

"I will go in with Josie," said Louis.

"Oh *thanks*," said Josic, taking his hand and giving it a squeeze.

Louis crawled in first with a torch to make sure there were no spiders. Josie went in next. He

looked at his little sister. She seemed so small and the house so big. He was just about to say "What are we doing?" when he realized that daylight was shining in.

Josie had the house balanced perfectly on her shoulders. It wasn't heavy but it was a bit difficult to walk and hold the house at the same time. Louis guided her carefully.

"A bit more this way... yes, you're doing fine."

Josie managed to walk the house down the street to where the very fussy woman who owned it was waiting.

"No, don't put it here, honey. I want it a bit more to the left," she said.

"Look," said Louis. "This is a three storey house my sister is carrying, not a beach chair."

Josie put the house down without breaking a single window pane.

"Cut," said the director. "That was just wonderful. The bit with your brother helping was so touching."

"It's in the bag, Josie," said Mr Two Suit. "The ad company were thrilled. In two days' time, we go to Hollywood!"

Louis and Josie were not thrilled. There had been no reporters to talk to so their plan hadn't worked so far.

"There'll be another chance tomorrow," whispered Louis. "Don't let's give up hope."

Their chance came sooner than they could have possibly imagined. There was a major disaster. One of the main support cables of the Brooklyn Bridge had come loose. Cars and buses were stuck, no one daring to move in case the whole bridge came down. The television was running all day bulletins. New York was brought to a standstill. In the Plaza Hotel, Josie and Louis sat glued in front of the screen.

"All those poor people," said Josie. "What will happen to them?"

"Oh, turn it off," said Mr Two Suit, "and let's get down to business. We have without doubt the silliest and easiest challenge of them all. This dad has contacted me and bet half a million dollars that you can't lift his son's rucksack. What a punk! It will be like stealing candy from babies."

"Why does he want me to do that?" said

Josie. "It sounds silly."

"Because he thinks one day your strength will give out. What a fool."

"But what about those people on the bridge?" said Louis.

"What about them? It means nothing to me. There's no money in people stuck on bridges."

"I'm going to get some sweets from the lobby. Are you coming, Louis?" said Josie.

Before Mr Two Suit had time to stop them, the phone rang.

"This is the plan," said Josie as they were going down in the lift. "I know it sounds a bit silly but I think I could help with that bridge."

Louis had been thinking the same thing until he had seen the pictures on TV. The bridge was an awesome size.

"Oh Josie, that really would be some trick," he said. "But are you sure?"

"Not really," said Josie, "but it's worth a go."

"It sure is," said Louis, smiling.

The lobby was full of people, all milling around, waiting for news about the Brooklyn

Bridge. Josie and Louis made their way to
the hall porter. They had decided that he
was their best bet because he had a kind,
understanding face. At first, he hadn't
the faintest idea what these two
kids were talking
about until it
finally sunk
in that the
little girl in
front of him
wanted to
help. He
nearly burst
out laughing,
then he looked at
Josie again. After
all, this was Josie

Jenkins, the little girl with the amazing
strength. Perhaps it wasn't such a silly idea
after all.

"What about your boss?" he asked.

Louis begged him not to tell Mr Two Suit

because if he knew that Josie was offering to do this out of the kindness of her heart, he would go bananas.

The hall porter looked quickly round the lobby, then he ushered them into a little room and told them to stay there until he got back.

Louis and Josie waited for what seemed like ages.

"I bet he's phoned Mr Two Suit. We'll be in big trouble," said Louis.

Just then the door opened and the porter reappeared.

"Don't say a word," he hissed. "Just do what I say. Mr Two Suit is on the war path, looking for you."

The porter hurried them out of the front of the hotel. To their amazement a helicopter had landed in the hotel grounds. Josie and Louis were rushed on to it and the door slammed to. As they rose high up into the sky, they could see the chubby little figure of Mr Two Suit waving his arms.

It gave Josie courage to see
him looking no bigger than
an ant.

16

Garth Griffen was in charge of the rescue services. So far he had the fire brigade, the police, ambulances and a number of helicopters at his disposal but nothing could be done. The whole thing was balanced on a knife edge. If they airlifted people off the Brooklyn Bridge, panic could break out. And if the balance was altered the whole bridge might collapse. And then there was the tide to think of. Garth Griffen was at his wits' end. The last thing he needed was an eight-year-old girl and her brother on the scene.

"This is a national disaster, not an adventure playground," said Garth.

"I am Josie Jenkins," said Josie very firmly.

Oh, he knew who she was all right. This was the girl with the mighty strength and the silly dresses. But a car was one thing – this was a huge bridge. Garth Griffen wasn't about to take any chances.

"What I need is some delicate lifting gear which should be here before the tide changes, not an eight-year-old girl," he said.

At that moment a call came through. There was a problem with the crane. It wouldn't be there for three hours.

"Oh great! Just great!" said Garth. "We don't have three hours. What we do have is a little girl!"

He looked again at Josie. This was madness. Heck,

he was a father of four. He knew all about girls. They could do many wonderful things but lifting Brooklyn Bridge? He doubted it.

"Look," said Louis. "I am not saying that she can do it, but surely it is worth a try."

Garth scratched the top of his head. Oh, what had he to lose? Nothing else seemed to be working.

Josie was put into protective clothing which was too big for her. So was Louis. "I don't leave Josie's side," he said.

"We're a team," said Josie proudly.

They were taken up to the top tower of the Brooklyn Bridge. Josie could see quite clearly where one of the suspension cables had given. Far down below the bridge was rocking dangerously back and forth in the wind. The cables were groaning loudly as if about to snap. It was all very scary.

Josie suddenly felt very unsure. The bridge was so massive. Would her trick be up to this?

Louis gave her hand a little squeeze. "Good luck," he said.

At that moment a whizz went down her
arms, even more powerful than the whizz
she had had when Billy Brand got his head
stuck in the railings.

Josie put her feet apart and got ready to
pull. Garth Griffen looked at this little girl
thinner than a runner bean, then back down
to the bridge. This was madness. He was just
about to say "Forget it, it's not going to
work," when he realized that little by little
Josie was pulling the slack cable until the
bridge was straight.

"Let's get those people off," ordered Garth, "and quickly."

The bridge was heavy, but not so heavy that she couldn't keep her grip. Far down below Josie could see the rescue services getting people to safety.

Louis kept saying encouraging things. "This is a pretty awesome trick, you know," he said. He had never been so proud of her.

Josie kept the bridge straight for a grand total of forty minutes. When she let go. everyone clapped and cheered. Garth Griffen put her on his shoulders and TV reporters rushed up to get the full story.

"How do you feel?" they shouted, pushing their cameras and microphones up to her face.

"I am pleased," said Josie, "that my trick has done some good." Then she carried on bravely, "Ever since I came over here, I have done nothing but silly things."

"But surely," said a lady reporter, "you are pleased with the fame and fortune that your challenges have brought you."

That was when Louis spoke up and told the reporter how they were nothing more than prisoners of Mr Two Suit.

"You did it!" said Josie. "You told everyone. Now Mum and Dad will come back and we will be able to go home."

But unfortunately Louis' appeal for help was cut due to the commercial break.

17

When they got back to the Plaza, Mr Two
Suit looked as if he might explode with rage.

"You go out of the hotel without my
permission and fix some piddling bridge
that I told you wasn't worth a dime, when
we could have made half a million bucks."

They were grounded; locked in their room
without supper, without television, nothing.
They both felt very down when the phone
rang. Josie answered it and to her

amazement
found that
she was
talking to
Stanley
Arnold.
He was in
Florida doing
a strong man
competition and he had turned on the news
and blow him down! there was little Josie
Jenkins. He was ringing to congratulate her
and to ask whether there was anything he
could do. She had only to ask.

Josie told him all about Mr Two Suit and
what had happened to Mum and Dad.

Stanley Arnold was a man of few words.

"I'll see you tomorrow, kids," he said.

18

The next morning Josie woke up and knew that something was different. She felt strange, heavy, as if her bones were made of lead. She got out of bed and then she knew. Her trick had gone, had disappeared as suddenly as it had come. She couldn't even lift the bedroom chair.

"I can't do it any more, Mr Two Suit," said

Josie. Mr Two Suit was not in a listening mood. He just wanted Josie looking pretty and down in the Palm Court in fifteen minutes.

"All you have to do is lift that little rucksack," he said.

Josie felt very small. She wanted Mum and Dad. She wanted to go home. When Louis came in, he found her in tears. The minute he looked at her, he knew that something had changed.

"Louis, my trick has gone," said Josie.

"It doesn't matter," said Louis. "At least you won't have to do any more stupid challenges."

Josie sobbed, "I tried to tell Mr Two Suit but he wouldn't listen. He said I had to be down in the Palm Court in fifteen minutes. What am I going to do?"

Louis wiped Josie's eyes. "Look, it was a great trick while it lasted," he said, "but you are much more than your tricks, Josie. Don't you see? Mr Two Suit can't do anything to us now. We'll be able to go home."

Josie brightened up. "You really think so?"

"Yes Josie, I do. I'm glad that your trick has gone away." And he took Josie's hand and together they went down to the Palm Court.

There they found a very tall, spotty lad, fifteen years old, with his very tall father. The rucksack was full of large, heavy encyclopedias. When Josie tried to lift it, she couldn't get it off the ground. There was a gasp of disbelief from the guests who had gathered round to watch. Mr Two Suit yelled, "Stop playing about and lift that rucksack!"

Just then Dad pushed his way to the front of the crowd. Josie couldn't believe her eyes. She ran towards him, tears rolling down her face.

"Dad, oh Dad, I can't do it any more."

"Never mind, princess," said Dad. "It doesn't matter. Come on, Louis, we're going home."

Dad lifted Josie up and took her to Mum who was standing at the back with Stanley Arnold. Louis and Josie had never been so pleased to see them.

"Oh thank you, thank you, thank you," Louis was saying to Mr Arnold.

"Very touching," said

Mr Two Suit. "Now if you would like to step this way, I think we have some serious talking to do."

Mum, Dad, Josie, Louis and Stanley Arnold followed Mr Two Suit into the lift up to their suite.

"I don't want him in the room," said Mr Two Suit, looking at Stanley Arnold.

"That's all right," said Stanley. "I'm waiting for a friend so I'll just stay in the corridor until he comes."

"We are going home," said Dad. "We have had enough of your monkey business. There was nothing in the contract about Josie losing her strength."

"Oh, very clever," said Mr Two Suit. "A short plane ride with Stanley Arnold and you are suddenly experts on contracts. You can leave and go home, by all means, when you have paid the bill."

"What bill?" said Mum. "Josie earned you lots of money. In fact, I think you might owe us something."

"Very funny," said Mr Two Suit, not laughing. "I have just written out a cheque for half a million dollars for a rucksack. And how much do you think staying in the Plaza costs? And your vacation in Florida, Josie's clothes, her hair, her food, her fitness trainer? Who do you think pays for that? YOU DO, you jerks."

He handed over a bill. "This is how much you owe me." Mum and Dad turned white. They had never seen so many noughts in their lives.

"There must be some mistake. I mean, we can't possibly owe this much," said Dad.

"Believe me, you do," said Mr Two Suit.

At that moment, Stanley Arnold entered the room. Behind him stood a very smart gentleman with tiny gold-rimmed glasses.

"May I introduce my lawyer?" said Stanley.

Mr Two Suit was about to say something but didn't. Stanley Arnold was, after all, very big and very strong. No one messed with Stanley.

"The contract if you please," he said. Mr Two Suit handed it over.

"I think," said the lawyer, looking hard at the piece

of paper, "that we will talk in the other room."

The Jenkinses and Stanley waited anxiously. They could hear raised voices, then all went quiet. They were in there for ages. Then the lawyer came back.

"There's bad news and there's good news," said the lawyer. "The good news is that you don't owe Mr Two Suit anything."

Dad and Mum gave a loud hip, hip, hurray.

"The bad news is that because it was a truly dreadful contract, he doesn't owe you anything either except your air fare home. I am sorry that I can't do more for you."

"Oh thank you," said Dad. "It doesn't matter about the money. We just want to be able to leave."

Stanley Arnold shook Josie's hand. "You are a very strong little girl with or without your trick, Josie Jenkins, and I wish you all the best. As for you, young man," he said, turning to Louis, "I take my hat off to you for looking after her so well."

"Hear, hear," said Mum and Dad.

Mr Two Suit booked them on to the very next plane to London. He couldn't wait to get rid of them. He had just heard news of a boy in Russia who could fly.

Josie sat in the lobby while Dad went to see if he could find a taxi. No more stretch limos.

"What are all these people doing?" said Mum. Louis looked at the crowd of people coming their way. He recognized the face of Garth Griffen. In the middle of the huge group was a very important-looking gentleman.

"May I introduce myself?" he said. "I am the Mayor of New York."

"Very pleased to meet you," said Josie politely, feeling a bit baffled. The mayor smiled. "On behalf of this great city, we would like to thank you for your bravery and for your selfless courage in saving so many from a possible disaster." A loud cheer went up. "To show our gratitude to you and your remarkable family, we would like you to accept this humble cheque as a sign of our appreciation."

Josie looked at the cheque in disbelief. There were even more noughts on it than on Mr Two Suit's bill. Josie jumped up with joy and gave the mayor a kiss. Cameras clicked.

"Thank you," she said. Everybody clapped.
It was quite a little party.

They were taken to the airport in the
mayor's own limousine and were flown first
class to London.

19

It didn't take long for everything to get back to normal. Josie was thrilled to see her house and her friends. She was even excited about going back to school. Billy Brand was pleased to see her and so was Mrs Jones. They all said that she had been missed. Dad and Mum were their old selves again and

Dad's customers forgave him for the late repairs on their cars.

Louis was just pleased that everything was how it used to be. It seemed to him that New York had been a dream except for one thing. He and Josie now got on really well and hardly ever fought. As for Josie, she didn't mind that she was no longer the strongest little girl in the world.

She didn't miss her trick one bit. She was glad to be plain Josie Jenkins, now eight but soon to be nine years old.

The Invisible Boy

To Dominic
With very happy memories of Splodge

"I can't believe it," said Mum, opening the gold envelope. "We won the top prize – a trip to the moon."

Dad, who was eating toast and reading the morning paper, said, "That's nice."

"Nice!" said Mum. "Charlie Ray, did you hear what I said? We have won a once-in-a-lifetime trip to the moon, all expenses paid, flying first class to Houston, then on the Star Shuttle, and staying in the Moon Safari Hotel, overlooking the Sea of Tranquillity. Oh Charlie, we are the first ones ever to have won this prize!"

Dad dropped his toast and paper.

"Let me see," he said. "Oh Lily my love, I don't believe it. We are going to the moon!"

Sam walked into the room to find his mum and dad dancing round the kitchen table and singing "Fly me to the moon and let me play among the stars."

"What's going on?" said Sam, who was only half awake and unused to seeing his parents singing quite so loudly on a Saturday morning.

They told him the good news, both excited and talking at once, so that it took quite some time before they realised that children under twelve weren't allowed. It meant quite simply that Sam couldn't go.

"Well, that's that," said Dad after Mum had phoned to double-check with Dream Maker Tours.

"I will be fine," said Sam bravely. "Look, you must go. It's only for two weeks and I have lots of friends I can go and stay with, like Billy. I'm sure his mum won't mind."

2

The great day arrived. Mum and Dad were packed and ready to go when the phone rang. It was Billy Brand's mother, who was terribly sorry to say that Billy was not at all well. The doctor had just come round and said he had a very infectious virus. Sam couldn't possibly stay with him now. Mrs Brand hoped it hadn't ruined their trip.

"What are we going to do?" said Mum, putting down the last of the suitcases.

"I don't know," said Dad.

Just then the doorbell rang. Dad answered it. He was surprised to find their next-door neighbour, Mrs Hilda Hardbottom, standing there.

"I just popped round to see if you wanted the plants watering while you were away," she said, smiling.

"That's very kind of you,

98

Mrs Hardbottom, but I don't think we will
be going after all," said Dad.

"What?" said Hilda, walking uninvited
into the hall and closing the front door
behind her. "Not going on a once-in-a-
lifetime trip to the moon! Why not?"

Mum felt a bit silly. She should have got
this better organised. "Sam's friend's mum
has just rang to say he's not at all well, so
Sam can't go to stay there," she said.

"Oh dear," said Mrs Hardbottom. "Still,
that shouldn't stop you. Anyway you can't
cancel, not now, with the eyes of the
world on you, so to speak."

"We really have no choice, I can't leave Sam alone," said Mum.

"We must phone Dream Maker Tours right away and tell them we can't go," said Dad.

"There is no need to cancel. If it comes to that I can look after Sam," said Mrs Hardbottom firmly.

Mum and Dad were lost for words. They felt somewhat embarrassed. Mr and Mrs Hardbottom were their neighbours, and had been for years, but they really knew nothing about them, except they kept to themselves and seemed nice enough.

It was Sam who broke the awkward silence.

"That's the answer, Dad," he said, trying to sound cheerful.

Mum and Dad looked at one another then at Sam. Oh, how they loved their little boy! It broke their hearts seeing him being so grown-up and courageous.

"It's very kind of you, Mrs Hardbottom, but…"

"Hilda," said Mrs Hardbottom, taking control of the situation. At that moment the doorbell rang. "No more buts," said Hilda, opening the front door as if it were her own house.

Plunket Road looked barely recognisable.
It was full of wellwishers and TV cameras.
Parked outside their front door was a
white shining limousine waiting to take
the Rays away.

A TV presenter with a games show
face walked into the hall where Mum and
Dad were standing. They both looked like
a couple of startled rabbits caught in the
headlights of an oncoming circus lorry.

"Mr and Mrs Ray, today is your day!
You are Dream Maker's out-of-this-world
winners!" said the presenter. "How does it
feel?"

Dad and Mum appeared to be frozen to the spot.

"Yes," said the presenter, "I too would be lost for words if I was lucky enough to be going to the moon."

Hilda spoke up. "They are a little sad to be leaving their son. But he is going to be fine, me and Ernie are going to look after him."

The camera panned on to Sam's face.

"You must be his kind and devoted granny," said the presenter, pleased at least that someone in the family had a voice.

"No," said Hilda, "I am the next door neighbour."

The presenter beamed his most plastic smile and his teeth shone like a neon sign. "Now isn't that what neighbours are for!" he said, putting an arm round Hilda and Sam.

Hilda was in heaven at being seen by forty million viewers world-wide. Mum and Dad smiled weakly. Nothing was agreed. This was all moving too fast.

"I brought round a disposable camera," Hilda continued. "I was hoping that my dear friends Charlie and Lily would take some nice pictures of the Sea of Tranquillity, for my Ernie. He wants to know what watersports they have up there on the moon."

"Well, isn't this cosy," said the presenter, handing the camera to Mum. He was now moving Mum and Dad out of the house into a sea of flashing camera lights, and somewhere in amongst all the chaos that was whirling around them, they found themselves parted from Sam. The white limousine whisked them away. The last thing they could see was Sam waving bravely.

There were two things at the top of Hilda Hardbottom's wish list. They had been there for forty years and hadn't until today shown any sign of coming true. The first was to be on TV, the second was to be rich.

"I don't know what's come over you, sweetpea, you hate boys," said Ernie in a stage whisper after Sam had gone to bed. "You always said they smelt of old socks that had been chewed by a dog."

"There is no need to whisper, Ernie Hardbottom, unless I say whisper," she snapped back at him.

Sam, who was trying to get to sleep upstairs in the cold spare bedroom with no curtains, heard Hilda's voice, and crept to the top of the landing to see what was going on. What he heard made going to sleep even harder.

"Because, you numskull, how else was I ever going to star on TV?" said Hilda. "You have videotaped it, haven't you?"

"Yes, every minute of it, dearest," said Ernie.

"Good," said Hilda. Then she added as an afterthought, "Sam's parents must have taken out a lot of travel insurance, don't you think?"

"Well, if they haven't, Dream Maker Tours would have done, I imagine," said Ernie, pressing the play button on the video machine.

"Just think if anything were to go wrong with that Star Shuttle! Think of all that insurance money," said Hilda, rubbing her hands together with glee.

"That's not very nice," said Ernie.

"Who said anything about being nice," said Hilda, a wicked grin spreading across her face.

Sam went back to his cold lumpy bed. Tears welled up in his eyes. Oh, how he hoped that nothing would go wrong and that his mum and dad would soon be safely home!

The next day Sam went back to school and only had to be with Hilda and Ernie in the evening. All the evenings were long and dull. There was never enough to eat. After tea they would all sit together watching TV, and Hilda would hand out some of her homemade treacle toffee. The first night Sam had been so hungry that he had made the mistake of taking a piece. To his horror his mouth seemed to stick together so he could hardly swallow, let alone speak. All he could do was sit there trying to finish the treacle toffee while listening to Ernie snoring and Hilda's stomach gurgling like an old dishwasher.

Bedtime couldn't come soon enough. Every night Sam would thank the stars that it was one day nearer to his mum and dad coming home.

But then, on the day his parents were due to return to earth, the unthinkable happened. Houston said they had lost all contact with the Star Shuttle. They were hoping it was just computer failure. The slow, mournful hours passed and the Star Shuttle still couldn't be found. Finally a spokesman for Dream Maker Tours announced on the six o'clock news that the Star Shuttle was missing.

5

The next morning Sam got ready to go to school. He would tell his teachers that he couldn't stay with the Hardbottoms any longer. He had lots of friends at school. He was sure someone would help him while this terrible mess was sorted out.

Hilda must have known what he was planning, for she was waiting for him by the front door, wearing her iron face. "Where do you think you're off to?"

"School," said Sam.

"No you're not. It's out of the question. Not at this sad time," said Hilda firmly.

"I can't stay here, I mean I was only supposed to be with you until my mum and dad got home," said Sam.

"Well, they're not home, are they, so it looks as if you're stuck with us," Hilda said smugly.

"But…" said Sam.

"The buts will have to make their own toast," said Hilda, pushing him back upstairs into his room.

The next few days passed in a haze. Hilda didn't allow him to go to school, or even out of the house alone, not with all the press and TV camped in their front garden. Sam Ray's parents were a hot story. Sam's picture appeared on every TV, newspaper, and Internet site in the world. Sam just remembered flashing lights and Hilda and Ernie being called the nation's favourite neighbours.

After a nailbiting week had passed, the officials at Houston said the Star Shuttle had been lost in space. All on board were presumed dead.

That was that. No more exciting pictures to be had. The TV and pressmen packed up and left.

Sam and his parents became yesterday's story. Old newspapers blowing around with the dead autumn leaves, and like them a thing of the past.

6

Hilda had liked the idea of being the nation's favourite neighbour and had made the most of it. She wore a kind and caring face that made the press and friends of the Rays say Sam was lucky to have Mr and Mrs Hardbottom to look after him. Especially as there were no living relatives.

But behind the thin disguise, Hilda was making plans. She had rented a cheap bungalow by the sea and made Ernie write a letter to Sam's school saying that they were taking Sam away on holiday, so that he would have a chance to get over his sad loss.

Hilda's plan was simple, and that was to get her hands on the Rays' insurance money. She wouldn't be able to do that if Sam said he didn't want to stay with them, and she couldn't keep him locked up forever. No, the best thing was to get right away. There were too many people offering to help. Mr Jenkins, who had mended Ernie's Ford Cortina, had said only the other week that he and his family would gladly look after Sam.

Ernie was a bit puzzled as to why Hilda was so keen to keep him.

"Why are you going to all the trouble and expense of booking a seaside holiday?" he asked. "We never go away."

"Because we can't stay here. People will begin to ask questions," said Hilda firmly.

"About what?" said Ernie scratching his head.

"About who is going to look after Sam," said Hilda beginning to lose her temper. "We don't want him saying he doesn't like it here."

"I'm sure he doesn't," said Ernie. "We can't look after him. We don't know anything about boys."

Hilda bristled like an old hairbrush. "I am only going to say this once more Ernie Hardbottom, and if it doesn't sink in to that sievelike brain of yours you can go and live in the potting shed with your CB radio for all I care."

Ernie looked at Hilda. She was not a pretty sight.

"The Rays," she said, talking to him as if he were five years old, "were insured for a lot of money by Dream Maker Tours, and now they are dead that money will go to Sam. Or to be more precise, to the guardians of Sam.

"If we play our cards right, that will be you and me."

"So we are going to adopt Sam," said Ernie, still not quite sure what Hilda was up to. "Don't you think, dearest, we are a little too old to be bringing up a boy?"

Hilda looked at Ernie as a cat might look at a mouse. "No," she said, "it means, you peabrain, that we are going to be rich."

"How do you make that out, sweetpea?" said Ernie, looking even more puzzled. "It's Sam's money, after all, and I don't think he would want to give it to us."

Hilda sighed. "I sometimes wonder how with a brain as small as yours you manage to keep going at all."

"That's not fair dearest," said Ernie in a small hurt voice.

"Oh, for pity's sake, life's not fair," said Hilda. "It is going to be our money and once we get our hands on it we are off to where the sun shines bright. Personally I am going to live the life I deserve. Sam can go whistle for his supper, and so can you if you don't buck up your ideas."

Ernie knew it was pointless to argue with Hilda. Once she got an idea in her head, it wasn't so much like watching a bull, rather a ten-ton lorry go through a china shop. Nothing was going to stop her.

7

That night Sam was unable to sleep. He looked out of his curtainless window at the back garden, with its neat rows of pumpkins, its potting shed, and its garden gnomes, lit up in the moonlight. He could even see the treehouse that Dad and he had made in his garden next door.

Sam flashed his torch up into the starry night sky. He had never felt more abandoned. Space seemed to him so everlastingly vast. Where did it end? He felt tiny and invisible.

Sam lay down and tried to get to sleep. Suddenly there was a loud crash outside. He sat up in bed. All was quiet in the house. Sam was sure that if it had been an important crash, Hilda and Ernie would be up in a flash, but nothing stirred. Sam looked out of the window again. Everything looked the same, except that something was glowing in the pumpkin patch.

Sam tiptoed past Hilda and Ernie's bedroom. The door was ajar and Hilda's snores were loud enough to cover the noise of the creaking stairs. He went down to the back door and managed with great difficulty to get it open. He felt somewhat stupid standing in the garden, in the middle of the night, in his slippers and pyjamas. If he was caught now he would be in big trouble.

He walked slowly down the garden path. There, among the gnomes and the prize pumpkins, was what looked like a metal salad washer. A little like the one Hilda used to clean lettuce in, but bigger and a lot fancier. Whirring sounds were coming from it.

Then, to his horror, a gust of wind
blew the back door shut. He turned the
handle, but it wouldn't budge. He was
locked out.

Things were not looking good. This is
most definitely a dream, thought Sam. For
there, walking about bowing to the garden
gnomes, was an alien with green and
splodgy skin, saying, "Hello, I come in
peas. Take me to your chef."

When the gnomes didn't reply, the little alien, who was only a bit bigger than them, adjusted the two long pink tufts that stuck out of the top of his head and started again. "Hello, I come in peas..."

"Can I help?" asked Sam.

The little alien looked up, not in the least bit put off by someone so much bigger than himself. "My name is Splodge," he said. "I am from Planet Ten Rings. I come in peas."

"Good to see you. I am Sam Ray," said Sam.

"Are you the big chef?" asked Splodge.

"No," said Sam, "I am just a boy. I don't cook."

Splodge looked at him and then said, "One milacue, please." He ran back to where the metal salad washer lay and went inside.

"If this is a dream," said Sam to himself, "then why does it all seem so real?"

"Chief," said the alien, coming out, "take me to your chief."

"If you mean Mrs Hilda Hardbottom," said Sam, "I don't think she would be too pleased to see you."

Splodge leant on a flowerpot and muttered to himself. Then, pointing to the garden gnomes, he said, "Who are all those people? Are they prisoners of the Bottom?"

"No," said Sam, "they are plastic, I think, and they don't talk. They are just there to decorate the garden."

Splodge started to make a funny noise
and for one awful moment Sam thought
he was choking. He was not up on alien
first aid. Then, to his great relief, he realised
Splodge was laughing. Sam began to laugh
too. Splodge went over to where a gnome
was standing and gently pushed him over.
He started to laugh again.

"Ssh," said Sam, who didn't want Hilda
and Ernie waking up. "Why are you here?"
he asked.

Splodge looked at him as if he had
asked about the silliest question going.

"Sauce of the tomato 57," he said.

This was crazy, thought Sam. "You mean tomato ketchup? You have travelled all this way for that?"

"Yes," said Splodge. "I have travelled from Planet Ten Rings to bring home sauce of tomato 57 for my mum as a present for her," he thought hard for a moment, "hello nice to see you day."

"Like a birthday," said Sam.

"What's that?" asked Splodge.

"Oh, you know, the day you were born," Sam said.

"That's it," said Splodge. "A birthday mum present."

"I think you might be in the wrong place," said Sam. "You need a supermarket." He pointed in the direction of the shops. "It's about a kilometre down the road."

Splodge bowed. "Thankyourbits," he said, walking back towards the metal salad washer.

"By the way, what's that?" asked Sam.

"A spaceship," said Splodge,
disappearing inside. The door shut behind
him. Sam waited, not quite knowing what
to do. The spaceship started flashing with
bright colours. There was an alarming
whooshing sound as it started to rise. It
hovered two metres off the ground and
then crashed back down again. Another
loud bang followed, the door slid open,
and Splodge came out bottom first. The
two tufts on the top of his head were
now knotted together.

"Cubut flibnotted," he said.

Broken?" asked Sam.

The little alien nodded. "Whamdangled,"
he said sadly. "I need to make spaceship
see-through."

"Do you mean invisible?" said Sam.
"How can you do that?"

Suddenly a light went on in the house,
and the curtains were pulled back to
reveal Hilda and Ernie, lit up like figures
in a toy theatre.

Splodge froze in fright. He had never
seen such a scary sight before.

"That's the Bottoms hard?" he said.

"Yes," gulped Sam.

He looked down at Splodge, but to his
surprise and alarm he had disappeared.
Sam felt very scared, standing there all
alone in the garden in the middle of the
night in his dressing gown and slippers.
How was he going to explain his way out
of this one? His legs began to shake. Then
to Sam's surprise he heard Splodge's voice.

"Hurry up," he said urgently, "it's invisible time."

"What?" said Sam. He couldn't see Splodge, but could feel something pulling on his pyjama bottoms.

"Hurry up," said Splodge again, "or you'll be whamdangled."

It was too late. The back door opened and there stood Ernie in his gumboots and Hilda in her rollers. She looked more frightening than any alien. She was flashing a torch round the garden. "I think it's that boy out there near the potting shed."

"Where?" said Ernie. "I can't see anything."

"That's because you are a short-sighted nincompoop," she hissed. "If that snivelling, smelly little toerag of a boy is out there he will be in big trouble."

"What are you doing?" said Splodge to Sam. "Now invisible time."

"I can't," said Sam desperately.

It was then that he felt Splodge press something onto his leg and the next thing he knew was that he was completely invisible, except for his slippers, which refused to disappear.

"I think you were seeing things," said Ernie, who just wanted to go back to his warm bed.

"I don't see things," said Hilda flatly. "Put your glasses on, and have a proper look.

Come on, I don't want to be standing out here all night."

"All right, all right," said Ernie, taking the torch from her. "Oh yes, I think I see something, sweetpea."

"What?" said Hilda, following Ernie.

Sam was frozen to the spot. His slippers seemed to shine out in the moonlight like a neon sign. Hilda and Ernie were moving straight towards him.

"I just…" started Sam.

Ernie looked round. "Did you say anything, dear?"

"Don't be daft, Ernie. Just keep walking," snapped Hilda.

It slowly began to dawn on Sam that
he really was invisible and it wasn't his
slippers that had caught Ernie's eye, it was
the spaceship. Sam started to walk quickly
back towards the open back door, his
heart thumping so loud that he was sure
that even if Hilda couldn't see him, she
could hear him. He went into the house,
Splodge still clinging on to his leg. Once he
was safely inside, Sam shut and locked the
back door.

10

Splodge stood in the kitchen tapping his foot. "See now you," he said impatiently to Sam, but all that could be seen of Sam were his dressing gown and slippers. Sam himself was completely invisible.

Sam was enjoying this and he was beginning to think that being invisible

might just be the answer to all his problems. He would now be able to escape from the Hardbottoms and get help. That was until he caught sight of himself in the hall mirror. There was nothing to see. How would anyone know he was Sam Ray if he was invisible?

Suddenly there was

a loud noise from behind him. Sam turned
round to see Splodge fiddling with a radio.
Sam quickly turned it off.

"Flibnotted! Fandangled! Need radio,"
said Splodge urgently, pulling one of his
tufts. "Must understand you better."

Hilda and Ernie were now banging
with all their might on the back door.

Sam picked up Splodge and went
upstairs to his room and got out his
Walkman. Splodge put one earpiece in
each tuft, then closed his eyes, folded his
arms over his fat little tummy and
listened. After a minute or two he started
singing at the top of his voice.

"Hip hop it never will stop,

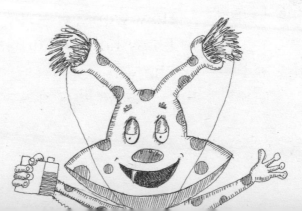

This planet can rock the stars.
Hip hop this never will stop.
We are the men from Mars."

"Not so loud," said Sam desperately to
Splodge, who said, "Like the music, dude, it
rocks. So tell me, why don't you know
how to do visible-invisible? Do you have
learning difficulties?"

"No," said Sam, "we humans don't do
that." He was beginning to feel a little
worried. "What did you put on me in the
garden?" he said.

"My one and only patch," said Splodge.
"I was going to use it on my spaceship,
but when I saw the Bottom hard, and
you not doing anything to escape, I did
what any other Splodgerdite would have
done, helped you out. Because, my H
bean, you had gone and forgotten how to
go invisible."

"No," said Sam, "I keep telling you we

humans don't do invisible."

"How do you live?" said Splodge with great feeling, as if this was a design fault that should have been mastered years ago. "It must be something awful to be seen all the time."

"It is," said Sam.

"To a Splodgerdite," said Splodge, yawning, "being invisible is like moving leglot. It's just what we do."

"Sorry," said Sam, "you lost me."

Splodge lifted one of his little legs and pointed. "Leglot."

"You mean leg," said Sam.

"Yes," said Splodge. "It's

easy peasy, once you get the handangle of
it. Like learning languages." He was now
making himself a bed in Hilda's old sock
basket. "Next day when the sun comes up
to see you," he said sleepily, "I get my
spaceship back."

"Will I be visible again tomorrow?" said
Sam, but Splodge was fast asleep.

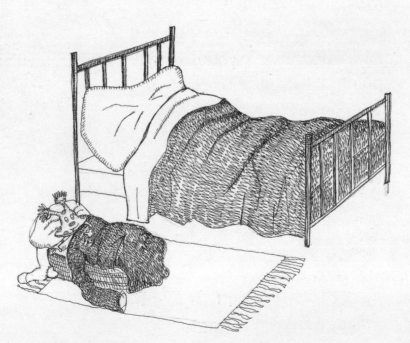

11

Sam woke to find he was quite normal again. He brushed his teeth, washed and got dressed, thinking all the time how wicked it would be if he was really invisible, and went downstairs for breakfast.

He was surprised to see that there were suitcases in the hall, and that Hilda was busy packing tins of food into boxes, which Ernie was taking out to the car. Perhaps,  thought Sam, they were leaving and he would finally be able to get away. It was then that he noticed that the back door had a panel missing from it. He was about to ask how that had happened, but the look on Hilda's face told him it wouldn't be a good idea.

"Now listen to me," she said, loading Ernie up with another box. "We are taking you to the seaside for a few days for a holiday."

"I don't want to go, I can't go," said Sam, feeling panicky. "I mean I don't want to leave my house, in case my mum and dad get back and can't find me."

"He's got a point, lambkin," said Ernie resting the box on the edge of the kitchen table. "Anyway, who's going to water my prize pumpkins?"

"You keep out of this, Ernie Hardbottom," said Hilda firmly. "Now you listen to me, young man. Your mum and dad are not coming back ever. The sooner you get that into your head the better."

Sam could feel tears burning at the back of his eyes.

"You should be grateful," said Hilda, picking up the metal salad washer and putting it on top of the box Ernie was carrying, "that we are going to all this trouble just for you."

"There's no need," said Sam desperately. "Why don't you go, and I can stay with a friend?"

Hilda's face twisted into that of a witch.

Sam wasn't going to cry in front of her. He looked again at the metal salad washer. He was sure he had seen it before.

"Where did you get this?" he asked, picking it up.

Hilda snatched it from him. "Stop fiddling, and get out of here before I box your ears, you ungrateful little scallywag." It was then that she let out a small scream. "What have you done to your ear?"

"Nothing," said Sam.

"Shouldn't boys have two ears, dearest?" said Ernie.

"Of course they should, peabrain." She pulled Sam over to the mirror. Sure enough one of his ears was invisible, although he could still feel it.

"Perhaps it fell off," said Ernie. "I think we'd better start looking for it, and then take him to the hospital to see if they can stick it back again."

"Shut up, Ernie, and take that box out to the car," said Hilda, looking at Sam carefully. "Are you playing games with me?" she said, reaching out to touch the missing ear. Sam moved away fast.

"I think Ernie's right, we should stay here," said Sam.

"Oh you do, do you?" said Hilda, folding her arms over her ample chest. "Well, I'm not fooled by your little joke. Now get upstairs and pack, and by the way, if you see your missing ear bring it with you."

12

Sam's only comforting
thought was that perhaps it
wasn't a dream, in which case he should
find an alien called Splodge sleeping in the
sewing basket. To his delight and great
relief, there he was, curled up into a ball.

"Good moon to you," said Splodge,
stretching out his little arms.

"We're off, come down here now,"
shouted Hilda.

"Is that the call of the Bottom hard?"
asked Splodge sleepily.

"Look," said Sam, "I don't want to go,
but they are taking me to the seaside and
I can't leave you here all alone."

"I can't leave my spaceship," said
Splodge, "so I suppose this is toodleoo."

"Then I've got bad news," said Sam. "It's
packed in the car that's taking me away.

Hilda thinks it's a salad washer."

Splodge sat up and looked at Sam. "That's a first rate spaceship," he said.

Hilda's voice had got louder and nastier. "If I have to come up and get you, there will be big trouble. Do you hear me, boy?"

Without another word Splodge got up, made his way over to the rucksack and climbed in. "The one good thing is that you're visible again," he said, making himself comfortable.

"Apart from one ear," said Sam, picking up his rucksack.

"What's an ear between aliens?" said
Splodge.

The Ford Cortina was packed to
bursting. Ernie was so small that he had to
sit on three cushions before he could see
over the wheel. Sam wondered why Hilda
didn't drive, as she was the one that gave
all the instructions.

"You are going too fast, keep over to
the left, no you shouldn't be in that gear."

All Ernie would say was a feeble, "Yes
dear, no dear."

It took the best part of a day to get
Skipton-on-Sea and when they finally
arrived, smoke was coming out of the

bonnet of the car. It came to a grinding halt
outside a dismal-looking bungalow that
smelt of damp and was colder inside than it
was out. Why anyone would come here for
a holiday was beyond Sam. His heart sank.

"This will do very nicely," said Hilda.

"Well," said Ernie, "the sea air must
agree with our Sam because look,
sweetpea, his ear is back again."

"Of course it is," snapped Hilda. "It was
only that smelly little toerag's idea of a
joke and I don't laugh that easily."

"No," said Ernie, "no, you don't."

13

It was hard to imagine a more miserable and isolated place. Even when tea was made and the lights turned on it had the feeling of being at the end of the world, and there was no way back.

Sam's room was smaller than the last one, and worst of all, the walls seemed to be made of paper. He could hear every word of what Hilda and Ernie had to say and none of it was good. Finally he could hear Hilda snoring, and he knew he was safe to look in his rucksack. He wanted to make sure he hadn't gone completely mad that morning imagining an alien, and a spaceship that looked like a salad washer. It was the only thing that had given him hope, as they drove farther and farther away from his home, from all that he knew and loved.

Sam emptied his rucksack carefully. There was no Splodge. He must have imagined it. He looked again. There were only the few things he had packed this morning. He turned it inside out. Tears started to roll down his face. He should have run away before they kidnapped him. Now Sam was lost just like his mum and dad.

He was lying in bed wondering, if he ran away, would he be able to find his way back, when the bedroom door opened all by itself.

Sam sat up in bed and flashed his torch. There, slowly making its way across the floor, without anyone helping it, was a bottle of tomato ketchup.

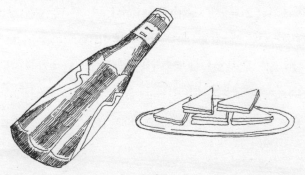

It came to a stop, and then Sam heard the padding of little feet and saw a plate of finger-size sandwiches wobbling in the air. They tottered one way, then another. Sam shone his torch on to the plate. A small voice said, "Stop it, I can't see."

"Is that you, Splodge?" said Sam hopefully.

"Who else," said Splodge, becoming visible again, with the plate of sandwiches in his hands. Sam had never been so pleased to see an alien before.

"These," said Splodge proudly, "are for you. Sandwiches of tomato ketchup and pea butter with nut."

Sam was so hungry that he ate them all down. They tasted great.

"Good news," said Splodge, "I have found my spaceship. Bad bit, wet inside."

"That's because Hilda thinks it's a salad washer," said Sam.

"It's a Viszler Junior Space Carrier," said

Splodge, sounding offended, "and that monster alien thinks it's a salad washer, whatever that may be."

"It's something you put lettuce in and then you whizz it around and hey presto you have clean lettuce," said Sam, finishing the last of the sandwiches.

"Or hay pisboo you have a broken spaceship," said Splodge.

"I'm sorry," said Sam.

Splodge didn't look up. He was busy, comforting himself by sucking the tomato ketchup out of the bottle.

For the first time since coming to stay with the Hardbottoms, Sam didn't feel alone. He sat on the bed with Splodge, looking out of the window. The moon looked like a big balloon that had come to rest on the garden wall.

Sam told Splodge about his parents' disastrous trip and how everyone thought they were dead and lost in space.

Splodge tutted. "I shouldn't think so, they most probably got stuck inside a grotter. Has anybody gone and looked?"

"What's that?" asked Sam.

"Surely you know what a grotter is," said Splodge.

"No I don't," said Sam. "I haven't a clue, what is it?"

Splodge looked worried. "Don't you learn anything at school then?"

"Maths, English, and history, mainly boring things like that," said Sam.

"Not about the planets, and the stars, and space dragons?" said Splodge. "Or how to look after a grotter, and what to do if an orgback turns up?"

"No," said Sam, who thought he would much rather learn about space than William the Conqueror.

"Grotters," continued Splodge, "are black as space and hard to see. They have huge tum tums and float about with their mouths wide open feeding on metricels of light, gaggerling up whatever gets in their way."

Sam looked at Splodge, still not understanding what he was talking about.

"Planet Ten Rings," explained Splodge," is milacue. So we look after the grotters and they look after us. Keep the orgbacks away, for a start."

"What are they?" said Sam.

"Humungous space monsters that can gaggerly up whole stars," said Splodge.

"Why don't you think an orgback swallowed the Star Shuttle then?" said Sam.

"Not possible, they live deep in space and we hardly ever see them. They wouldn't be bothered with a smidger of a thing like a spaceship. It wouldn't be worth munching."

"Would a Star Shuttle be all right inside a grotter or would that be the end of it?" asked Sam anxiously.

"More likely to make a grotter tum feel all wobbly and wonky," said Splodge. "I need to get a message home to my mum and dad. Then I would be able to tell them about the Star Shuttle."

But the problem was, how were they going to do that, now Splodge's spaceship was broken.

15

The morning did not bring with it a cheerful picture of holiday bliss. Thin drizzle fell and Sam could not see the sea because of a cement wall that blocked out the view. All the neighbouring bungalows were boarded up.

Hilda was busy trying to sort out the kitchen. "Did you get up in the night and take some food?" she said in a menacing voice.

"No," said Sam.

"Well, there are breadcrumbs where breadcrumbs shouldn't be," said Hilda.

"Perhaps there's mice," said Sam.

Hilda picked up the broom and shook it at Sam. "I don't want any more of your cheek, you little toerag. Go out and play."

"It's raining," said Sam.

"Out!" shouted Hilda.

Sam went out into the back yard. You couldn't call it a garden. It had high walls and crazy paving, and looked more like a prison yard. In it were two broken garden chairs, a washing line with a mouldy dishcloth hanging from it, and a pot with some tired plastic flowers sticking out of it.

Ernie was in the tiny shed at the back, fiddling about with wires.

"What are you doing?" asked Sam.

Ernie nearly jumped out of his skin. "Nothing, dear, nothing," he said. "Oh, it's you. What do you want?"

"It's raining," said Sam.

"Oh all right, you can stay here, but don't fiddle," said Ernie.

"What's that?" asked Sam, pointing to a funny-looking machine.

"It's a citizen's band radio," said Ernie, beaming with pride as he showed Sam how it worked. "It's not like your everyday radio. Before I retired I used to

drive long distance lorries, and this is how
we talked to each other. We all had
different names." Ernie blushed and said,
"I was called Tiger Raw. Sometimes if I
was lucky, I would be able to pick up
signals on it from as far away as Russia
and beyond. Isn't she beautiful!"

"Could it send messages into space?"
asked Sam eagerly.

"I don't rightly know," said Ernie,
scratching the top of his head. "That's a

mighty long way away, isn't it. I mean, it's farther than Russia."

"Only a little bit," said Sam.

"Anyway, I've just bought a bigger receiver," said Ernie, "but I'm having trouble wiring it up. The instructions seem to be written in double Dutch," he said sadly, looking at the manual.

"Ernie, where are you?" shouted Hilda.

"Out here, sweetpea," called Ernie.

"What are you doing?"

"Nothing, dearest, just fiddling," said Ernie.

"Stop it right now," shouted Hilda, "and come in here and help me make pea soup. And you too," Hilda shouted at Sam.

An awful smell of overcooked vegetables greeted them as they walked into the kitchen.

"I want you to stir this," said Hilda, showing Sam a pot of smelly, slimy green liquid. "Don't let it stick to the bottom. That soup is going to have to last us a week."

Sam sighed, and did as he was told. It was then that he realised both his hands were going invisible.

"Hilda," said Ernie, staring at Sam, "do you think boys fade away when they are unhappy?"

"What gibberish are you talking now, Ernie?" said Hilda.

"Sam's hands. They've gone and vanished," said Ernie.

Hilda turned on Sam. "You are doing this on purpose, aren't you, you ungrateful boy, and after all the trouble that we've gone to!"

"I just want to go home," said Sam bravely. "I shouldn't be here."

"He's got a point, dearest," said Ernie.

Hilda looked more frightening than an old flesh-eating dinosaur, all red and furious. "You keep out of this, you peabrain," she snapped, towering over Sam. "You'd better stay in your room until you learn not to play any more of these jokes, or you'll be sorry you were ever born."

16

Splodge was on the bed, listening to Sam's Walkman, and finishing off the last of the tomato ketchup.

"The good news," said Sam, sitting down next to him, "is that Ernie has a radio and a powerful receiver which he can't work. It just might get a message back to your planet. The bad news is, I'm grounded until my hands become visible again."

"It's going to be a long time then," said Splodge.

Sam was slowly fading away. By teatime he was completely invisible. All that could be seen of him were his clothes.

"I don't think I should have stuck that patch on you, " said Splodge anxiously. "It was meant for spacecraft, not for H beans."

"Stop worrying," said Sam. "Look, last time I came back, so why wouldn't it happen again?"

Splodge tried explaining about invisibility, but it was no use, Sam was far too excited, working out the best combination for frightening the pants off Hilda Hardbottom.

"Hi," he said calmly, walking into the kitchen for tea. "I am so hungry I am almost fading away."

Ernie and Hilda nearly jumped out of their skins when they saw a cap and a pair of trousers coming towards them.

"I don't think this is right, dearest," said Ernie, dropping the newspaper. "Shouldn't we be able to see him?"

"Of course we should," said Hilda shakily.

"I think it might be best to take him home, and get a doctor to have a look at him," said Ernie.

"What do you think would happen, you ninny, if we went home with an invisible boy?" said Hilda,

"I don't know, sweetpea," said Ernie.

Hilda sat down at the kitchen table. She was really worried. This wasn't in her grand plan. In fact she could be accused of causing Sam's disappearance. Then they would be in deep trouble. Hilda couldn't allow her plan to go wrong, not now when she was so close to getting what she wanted. Maureen Cook from Dream Maker Tours had said it was only a matter of her seeing Sam, then the money would be as good as theirs.

"Remember the ear, sweetpea, it came back," said Ernie, trying to sound encouraging.

Hilda filled their bowls with green slimy pea soup.

"Eat up," she said, putting on her TV face, "we don't want you fading away altogether now, do we."

Sam took off his cap and put it on the table. Hilda jumped back. There was now nothing to show that Sam was sitting in his seat, except a spoon playing with the slimy soup.

"I don't much like pea soup," said Sam, who was enjoying seeing Hilda squirm.

"What do you like?" said Hilda nervously. "You can have anything you want as long as it helps make you visible again."

So Sam gave her a long list, starting with twelve small bottles of tomato ketchup.

17

That night Hilda couldn't sleep. She was walking up and down in the lounge when a picture came off the wall right in front of her, and a china dog started to move across the mantelpiece. Sam was having fun.

"Is that you, Sam?" she said in a shaky voice. Sam didn't answer. Splodge, who was also invisible, was tickling her leg. She let out a scream and Ernie came in, yawning. What he saw made his legs wobbly with fright. A chair was floating round the room.

"That's not right," said Ernie, "I mean, chairs don't do that, do they?"

The chair dropped to the ground with a thud.

"Of course they don't, you ninny," Hilda said trembling.

"You know, sweetpea," said Ernie, "I think this place might be haunted. I just felt a rush of cold air." The lounge door closed with a bang.

Hilda recovered herself. "Of course it's not haunted," she snapped, picking up a cushion and hitting out at thin air. "Take that, you little toerag," she shouted. But Sam and Splodge had left, and were safely out of the way in the shed.

"I like being invisible," said Sam. "The only drawback is that it's chilly without your clothes on."

"Pish bosh, you're supposed to come and go, not stay like that all the time," said Splodge. "The sooner we get a message home the better."

The CB radio was not working that well, mainly because it had been wired to the receiver the wrong way. It took

Splodge some time to get it sorted out.

"Come on," said Sam, "I'm getting chilly out here."

"Well go back to the monster grotto then," said Splodge, "and make us something to fill up gurgling tummy."

The radio was now making strange noises and Splodge kept moving the knobs  and listening. Then he started speaking in a language that Sam couldn't understand.

"Χαλλινγ Πλανεντ τεν ρινγσ"

Sam walked back towards the bungalow. The lounge looked as if a giant hippo had had hysterics. Hilda had finally gone to bed exhausted, and was snoring like a battleship attacking her enemy.

The great thing about being invisible,
thought Sam, opening the fridge and
looking inside, is that I don't feel frightened
any more. I have some power and that is a
truly wicked feeling. He poured out all the
milk there was into two glasses, made a
pile of peanut butter sandwiches and
found the last bottle of tomato ketchup.

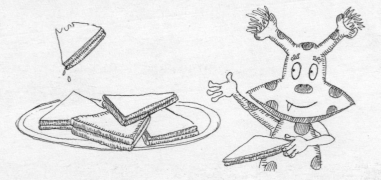

"I've got message home," said Splodge,
becoming visible again. "They've heard of
a sick grotter, in fact it's caused quite a
hollerburluke. Something is definitely
stuck inside it. They're on their way out to
it. Also my mum says not to worry and
sends you her toodle hyes."

"Oh that's wonderful," said Sam.
"So what will happen now?"

"Mum and Dad want to say hi and talk
to me again tomorrow. Also I've got to tell
them about the invisible problem,"
mumbled Splodge. "I'm sure my dad
and mum can think of something."

18

The bungalow was unusually quiet the next morning. Hilda had taken the car into the village to do some shopping, and Ernie was in the shed, playing with his radio. To his delight it was working better than it had ever done before, picking up some very strange sounds, "Χαλλινγ σπλογε σπαχε σηυττλε ρχοϖερεδ αλλ ον βοαρδ αρε σαφε."

Sam and Splodge spent the best part of the morning in the lounge. Sam was still invisible, but today he was dressed. It was too chilly to walk about without your clothes on. They sat together on the beaten up sofa, eating cereal out of the packet, watching whatever they wanted on TV.

Ernie, who had been left with strict instructions not to let Sam out of his sight, kept coming in from the shed, and saying, "You all right then?" On one of these visits he was sure he saw a green spotty little fellow sitting next to Sam, but then again he might just be seeing things, he hadn't got his glasses on, and the next time he looked it had gone.

About two o'clock the phone rang. Ernie picked it up. It was Maureen Cook from Dream Maker Tours. She couldn't have sounded more helpful, and said she would be coming down to see Sam tomorrow, to talk about his future.

"That will be nice," said Ernie, putting down the phone and telling Sam what she had just said.

"Do you think she will recognise me?" asked Sam.

"Oh dear," said Ernie. "Oh dear, I forgot you were invisible."

Hilda was not in a good mood when she arrived home at teatime, weighed down by shopping bags. Her mood was not improved one little bit when Ernie told her about Maureen Cook. She started rumbling like an old boiler ready to burst.

"You are worse than hopeless, you peabrain," she said to Ernie, who was looking very sheepish. "What are we going to show her, an invisible boy?"

"Perhaps," said Sam, "if you were kind to me, I might become visible again."

"It's worth a try," said Ernie in a small shaky voice.

Hilda said nothing, but banged and thumped round the kitchen unpacking the shopping.

"Oh that looks nice, sweetpea," said Ernie, seeing all the things Sam had asked for, including the twelve bottles of tomato ketchup.

"Well, none of it's for you," she snapped at Ernie. "It isn't you that's invisible, more's the pity." She handed Sam a bag. "Put these on," she ordered.

In it were a woolly balaclava, a pair of multi-coloured gloves, a cheap pair of dark glasses, and as the finishing touch, a pair of plastic joke lips.

"What are these for?" said Sam, laughing.

"This isn't funny," said Hilda. "Just do as I say."

When he saw himself in the hall mirror he couldn't stop laughing. Oh, now he really did look scary, as if he were about to rob a bank. Roll on tomorrow, he thought. How was Hilda going to get out of this mess?

19

The reason, Splodge said, that Splodgerdites adored tomato ketchup was simple. It was the sauce of their good looks, it kept them young, healthy, and wise. Also,

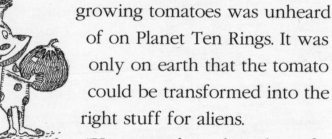 growing tomatoes was unheard of on Planet Ten Rings. It was only on earth that the tomato could be transformed into the right stuff for aliens.

"Have you been here lots of times, then?" asked Sam.

Splodge looked down at his toes. "No," he said, "I have only been here once before with my dad, and it was a short sort of visit."

It turned out that Splodge was only about as old as Sam, and that this was the first time he had travelled on his own to earth.

"I thought I would get my mum a present," said Splodge sadly, "but it all went a bit starshaped. I am only a junior space flyer, I start my AST course next year."

"What's that?" asked Sam.

"Advanced Space Travel," said Splodge. "That's when we learn everything to do with space and all the other things like grotters and orgbacks."

Sam didn't like to ask, he had a nasty feeling he already knew the answer.

"Have you ever used one of those invisible patches before?" he said.

"No," said Splodge.

"Do you know what happens when one of those patches is put on a boy like me?" asked Sam.

"No," said Splodge, looking a little shamefaced. "They are only to be used when everything is whamdangled."

Sam was beginning to feel panicky. It was one thing to be invisible for a few

days, but not forever. What if his parents
came back? How would they know it was
Sam if they couldn't see him?

"Will I ever be visible again?" asked
Sam anxiously.

"Need to speak to Dad," said Splodge.
"I'm sure someone on Ten Rings will
know what to do."

But it was proving to be
quite difficult to get a message home.
Ernie had been fiddling again with the
radio and it took Splodge ages to pick up
a signal, and then he could hardly hear
what they were saying, except for the odd
word like σουνδ σηυττλε σαφε.

"We'll have to try again tomorrow," said
Sam, seeing the look on Splodge's face. He
was tired and his bright green skin was
losing its shine.

"Pish bosh, I want to go home," he said
sadly. "I miss my mum."

"I know," said Sam. He took Splodge
back to the house, gave him a bottle of
tomato ketchup and tucked him up in bed.

"So do I," said Sam quietly. "I miss Mum
and Dad very much indeed."

20

The next day the Hardbottoms were up early, cleaning and tidying the bungalow.

Hilda put on her smiling face that she kept at the bottom of an old make-up bag and only used for special occasions. Ernie put on his one and only suit. The tea had been set out on a tray in the lounge, and the curtains were drawn. Hilda had put

Sam in the armchair with a rug over his knees. When Ernie saw him sitting there in the balaclava and dark glasses and false lips, he jumped with fright.

"Hilda," he said, "there's a strange man sitting in the armchair.

He wasn't there a moment ago. Did you let him in? He looks very scarey!"

"That, you peabrain, is Sam," said Hilda.

When Maureen Cook arrived she was rather taken aback by the Hardbottoms' idea of a holiday. The bungalow was seedy, and smelt damp.

"You could have taken yourselves somewhere nice and hot," she said. "We would happily have paid."

"Didn't want to look too greedy," said Hilda, smiling. "Not until all this is settled, so to speak."

"Please remember," said Maureen, "Dream Maker Tours are here to make your dreams a reality."

"I hope so," said Hilda, taking Maureen through to the lounge, and placing her in the chair furthest away from Sam. Hilda handed her a cup of tea and a piece of cake, talking all the time, like a car alarm that wouldn't stop, about how much they cared for Sam and how he enjoyed sitting in the dark wearing a balaclava.

"It makes him feel protected from the outside world. Grief," said Hilda, "can do strange things to one."

"Please Mrs Hardbottom," said Maureen, "will you let me speak. Are you feeling all right, Sam?" she asked.

"As I said," interrupted Hilda, "Sam is a bit shy."

Sam nodded and mumbled, "I'm OK."

"Do you like it here?" Maureen started.

Hilda interrupted again. "These questions aren't too strenuous, are they?" she said, sounding concerned. "It's just that we care so much for the boy, and want to protect him. After all, I'm not called the Nation's Favourite Neighbour for nothing."

"Quite so," said Maureen, bringing a picture of Sam out of her briefcase, and going over to the window to draw back the curtains. "I would like to see your face,

Sam, if you don't mind."

"I do mind," said Hilda, rushing past her
and standing in front of the window. "He
has been through an awful lot, why does
he have to answer these questions? Isn't it
enough that he's here?"

"I am just doing my job, Mrs
Hardbottom," said Maureen wearily. This
wasn't going to plan. She had hoped to
have all this sorted out in no time at all.

"Treacle toffee," said Hilda, holding out
a sweet tin. "I made it myself."

Maureen smiled weakly. "Well, one
piece if you insist, then I must ask Sam
these questions."

Sam watched the look of horror spread
over Maureen Cook's face as her jaws

slowly stuck together and she was unable to say another word.

Hilda took her back to the chair farthest away from Sam.

"Shall we talk about the money?" said Hilda, smiling charmingly.

At that moment Ernie came into the room. "Wonderful news, sweetpea," he said. "The Star shuttle has made contact with Earth. I just heard it on my CB radio. It looks like Mr and Mrs Ray will be coming home after all."

"Hooray!" shouted Sam, sending the false pair of lips shooting across the room.

Maureen looked startled and Sam put his gloved hand across his mouth and said, "It's the best bit of news ever."

21

Maureen Cook had written out a cheque to cover their holiday expenses.

"Is that all?" said Hilda, seeing how little she had been given.

But Maureen was now running towards her car, still unable to speak, a hanky held over her mouth.

"Wait a minute, come back," shouted Hilda.

It was too late. Maureen sped off down the road at top speed.

"It's all your fault," Hilda screamed at Ernie. "If you hadn't come charging in like that, we would have been given loads of money."

Hilda marched like an invading army into the shed. She got hold of the CB radio, and lifted it high above her head.

"Don't do that!" shouted Ernie and Sam together. It was too late. Hilda threw it to the ground.

"I think," said Ernie sadly, "you've gone and broken it."

"I hope so," said Hilda. "If you had half a brain, you would have seen what I was trying to do instead of mucking up all my plans."

Hilda went back into the kitchen followed by Sam. All that could be seen of him now was a pair of dark glasses.

"You wretched boy, none of this would have happened if you hadn't gone invisible," yelled Hilda. "Well, you can stop playing games. I haven't come this far for you to ruin everything. You are going to become visible again and tell your mum and dad you had a lovely time with us.

Do you hear me?"

Sam, who had long lost his fear of Hilda, said calmly, "I won't. I will tell them the truth, that you are a mean, nasty two-faced witch."

Hilda grabbed a broom. "What did you call me?" she shouted, bringing it down with a nasty crack on the sunglasses, which fell broken to the floor.

At that moment Splodge walked into the room, quite visible.

"I agree," he said.

Hilda dropped her broom and scrambled up on the table as fast as her tubby legs would let her. Splodge went over to where the broken glasses lay, and picked them up.

"You," said Splodge, "should be boggled."

Hilda started screaming at the top of her voice.

Ernie came in holding his smashed radio.

"Look!" yelled Hilda, pointing at Splodge. "It's a monster, a rat, an alien. Don't stand there, do something!"

If Ernie wasn't mistaken, this was the same little fellow that he had seen sitting with Sam the other day on the sofa.

"Well, what are you waiting for? I think that creature has murdered Sam!" said Hilda "Look at the smashed glasses."

Ernie said nothing. He had seen many frightening things in his life, though sadly none of them as frightening as his wife when she was in one of her moods.

"I can't see what all the fuss is about," said Sam, invisible from the other side of the room. "That's my friend Splodge, from Planet Ten Rings, and he's not best pleased that you have ruined his spaceship by filling it with water."

Hilda went white with fright. "Do something, Ernie," she pleaded.

For the first time since he had married Hilda, way back in the dark ages, Ernie felt brave. If a boy and a little alien could stand up to her, so could he.

"No, I won't," he said firmly. "You have gone too far this time, Hilda. I should have had the courage to stop you, but I didn't – more's the pity."

Splodge stepped forward. "You are a cruel and mean hard bottom, and you give earth H beans a bad name," he said, holding his little hands out before him. Bright green rays came out of his fingertips. Hilda's face went a horrid pink and then became covered in tiny green spots.

"Nice one," said Sam.

Hilda quickly climbed down off the table, ran into the hall, grabbed her coat and hat, stuffed the cheque into her handbag and ran out of the front door and down the street as fast as her stumpy legs would carry her.

22

On the TV that night, every programme
was about the Star Shuttle's miraculous
return to earth. Experts were talking about
black holes and all sort of other theories to
explain how a spaceship could go missing
for so long. No one mentioned grotters or
a small planet called Ten Rings.

Splodge had been spending the evening
trying to wire the radio up to his
spaceship in the hope of getting a message
home, but it wasn't working. Ernie was
out in the back yard with the receiver.

"Try it now," said Ernie.

There were a few beeping noises and
then nothing.

"Pish bosh, it's hopeless," said Splodge
sadly. "We are truly boggled."

"Often when things don't work," said
Sam "my dad gives them a little tap. He
says it helps them wake up."

"Go on then," said Splodge.

Sam tapped the top of the spaceship.
Nothing happened.

"Well," said Splodge, "it doesn't work."

But that was as far as he got. The
spaceship suddenly lit up. Sparks of
rainbow colour came shooting out of it,
lighting up the drab back yard.

"OW!" said Sam.

Then they all heard

Τηισ ισ πλανεντ τεν Ρινγσ Χαλλινγ Σπλοδγε

"That's my dad!" shouted Splodge.
"That's my dad!"

It was a much larger spacecraft that
landed in the back yard that night, and
Splodge's parents were thrilled to see their
son.

"This is Sam," said Splodge, looking
down at his toes. Sam held out the arm of
his old jumper.

"Oh dear," said Splodge's dad. "What
have you done, junior?"

"He was trying to protect me," said Sam.

"He didn't realise I couldn't go invisible."

"Sorry, Dad," said Splodge.

His dad smiled a kind smile. "Well, we'd better put it right."

He held out his hands and a blue light flashed around Sam. The next thing, there he was, visible again.

"Thank you," said Sam. "Oh, it's great to be seen again."

Ernie offered to make them tea, but Splodge's parents wanted to get home as soon as possible.

"Wait a minute, I can't go without Mum's present," said Splodge.

He rushed back into the bungalow and brought out twelve bottles of tomato ketchup.

"These are for you, Mum," said Splodge.

She gave him a hug, then thanked Sam for looking after him so well. "He's a bit young to be doing this," she said, waving goodbye. Sam wanted to thank Splodge's parents for helping him find his mum and dad, but there was no time. He was interrupted by the noise of police cars screeching down the road. Splodge just had time to wave before the doors of the spaceship closed behind him. Then there was a whirling noise and in a shower of lights and glitter they were gone.

The police were now knocking loudly on the front door. "Mr and Mrs Hardbottom," they shouted, "open up in the name of the law."

23

It was the best homecoming ever. Mum
and Dad were over the moon to see their
beloved boy. They couldn't have been
more proud of Sam, and how well he had
coped under such appalling circumstances.
It was hard to believe that Hilda could
have turned out to be so cruel and horrible.

It had been Maureen Cook who had
alerted the police. They had arrived just in
time to see sparks coming from behind
the garden wall.

They had driven Sam home in style to
his parents, the blue lights flashing all the
way to 2 Plunket Road.

Ernie had been taken away for questioning, while Hilda was caught trying to get on a flight for Majorca. It was her pink face with its green spots that had given her away.

Mr and Mrs Hardbottom were both charged with abduction and trying to take money under false pretences.

The Comet

The neighbour from hell

Hilda had at last found the fame she had been looking for. Her picture appeared on every newspaper, with the caption "The neighbour from hell." She was sent to prison. Ernie was let off with a caution. The judge felt that if he hadn't been so frightened of his wife he wouldn't have gone along with her plan.

Mum and Dad felt relieved that it was all over, and they were just happy to be back on earth with Sam.

The funny thing was they had no memory at all of what happened to them, except of falling asleep on the homeward journey and waking up again as they were landing. Everyone on board had been most surprised to find out that anything had been wrong, or that they had been missing for so long. Even the officials at Houston agreed that the space shuttle disappearance was a mystery.

"It's like it became invisible," said one Houston scientist.

Sam kept quiet about Splodge. Who would believe him? At her trial Hilda had gone on about aliens, and how boys couldn't be seen, only heard. Everyone thought she had gone barmy.

After it was all over, Ernie lived quietly next door, pottering in his garden. One evening while Sam was kicking a football round, Ernie leaned over the fence and said to him, "There's something that really bothers me."

"What?" said Sam.

"That little fellow Splodge, he asked me something as I was helping him with the radio. He said did I know the meaning of 57 varieties? Do you think," said Ernie, "that he was talking about space and the universe?"

"Tomato ketchup," said Sam.

Ernie looked puzzled.

"That's what it says on the ketchup bottle, 57 varieties," said Sam, and they both burst out laughing.

The Boy Who Could Fly

For Dominic
with all my love

Mrs Top opened her front door one grey Wednesday afternoon to find a Fat Fairy standing there.

"Is this 6 Valance Road, and are you Thomas Top's mother?" asked the Fat Fairy.

Mrs Top looked a little taken aback.

"Yes," she said, "but I think there must be some mistake. The birthday party has had to be cancelled."

The Fat Fairy adjusted her glasses and huffed.

"Well. I have got it written down here that I am booked for today, the fourth of May, at three o'clock for Thomas Top's ninth birthday," said the Fat Fairy firmly.

"And I never get it wrong."

"I don't understand. I didn't book anyone for Thomas's party. I mean, we always have Mr Spoons the magician. I never asked for a fairy," said Mrs Top.

"No one ever does, dear," said the Fat Fairy, "we are supposed to be a surprise."

Mrs Top was beginning to feel quite flustered.

"You see the party isn't happening today because Thomas is ill," she said. "We had to put it off. He's going to have it on the same day as his dad's birthday now."

"Well, that is nothing to do with me," said the Fat Fairy. "I am here just to wish him a happy birthday. It says nothing about entertainment or parties."

"Oh I see," said Mrs Top, feeling relieved, "you are some sort of singing telegram. I can't think who sent you."

"I wouldn't worry about it," said the Fat Fairy, smiling.

204

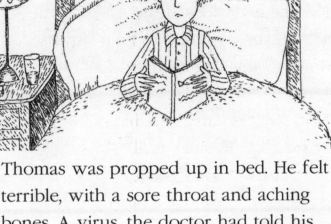

Thomas was propped up in bed. He felt
terrible, with a sore throat and aching
bones. A virus, the doctor had told his
mum. He was to stay in bed until he felt
better, and today was his birthday and he
felt worse.

So far he had been given a book on
fishing for beginners from his dad, a pen
from his mum, a brown jumper from his
Aunt Maud, and a pound stuck with
masses of sticky tape to an old Christmas

card from his Uncle Alfie. Things were not looking good when suddenly his mum entered the room, with the fattest fairy he had ever seen.

She had bright pink hair and was wearing a tutu two sizes too small. Her wings were lopsided and it looked as if she had sat on her tiara. If Thomas hadn't been feeling so unwell he would have burst out laughing.

"It's a surprise," said his mum anxiously.

The Fat Fairy looked around the room and huffed, then went and sat on the end of Thomas's bed.

"I wouldn't get too close to him," said Mum. "He could be infectious."

The Fat Fairy took no notice and said in a mournful voice, "Love a cup of tea, dear."

Mrs Top went downstairs, saying she wouldn't be a minute.

"Not much of a birthday," said the Fat Fairy, looking round Thomas's room and at his presents.

"Why are you here?" said Thomas.

"To give you a birthday wish," said the Fat Fairy.

"You're joking, aren't you?" said Thomas.

"No," said the Fat Fairy. "Come on, just tell me what your wish is, and then I can be on my way."

"I don't know," said Thomas. He wasn't sure what to make of her. "This is just a game, isn't it?"

"It's no game," said the Fat Fairy. "Come on, let's get this finished with before your mum comes back with tea and fairy cakes."

"I wish I was..." said Thomas.

"No good," interrupted the Fat Fairy. "You can't wish for all the money in the world or to turn Aunt Maud into a sheep. It just won't work like that. You have to wish for something like having the most beautiful hair or being able to sing like a cherub, or being a whizz at computers. Now do you get it?"

Thomas looked at her again. "Mum doesn't have any fairy cakes," he said.

The fairy shrugged her wings. "Come on, come on," she said. "Concentrate, it's not every day you get a wish granted."

"You're kidding, right?" said Thomas.

"Whatever," said the Fat Fairy. "Just get on with it."

"I wish that..." said Thomas.

"No good," the fairy interrupted. "You

can't wish for your father to be fun. It has to do with you, Thomas," she said gently. "After all, today is your ninth birthday."

Thomas looked surprised. "How did you know I was going to wish for that?" he said.

"Quick," said the Fat Fairy as Mum's footsteps could be heard coming up the stairs.

Thomas said the first thing that came into his head. "I wish I could fly." Why he said that he couldn't think.

"Nice one," said the Fat Fairy, standing up just as Mum entered the room with two cups of tea and a plate of fairy cakes.

"I'm all done and dusted, dear," said the Fat Fairy, giving a loud belch. "All this wishing plays havoc with my insides," she went on, gulping down the tea and putting three fairy cakes in her handbag. "Well, I can't stay here all day enjoying myself."

And without so much as a goodbye,

she made her way down the stairs. Mum followed, saying, "Wait a minute, I was wondering which company sent you," but by the time she had made it to the front door the Fat Fairy had vanished.

Thomas went back to school the following Monday.

Monday was his worst day. There were games and Thomas hated games. "Could I have a note saying that I've been ill?" he asked his mum.

"No," said his dad firmly. "If you are well enough to go back to school, young man, you are well enough to play games."

"I think, Alan, that's a bit hard," said his mum. "He has been very unwell."

"I am not having that boy mummy-coddled any more," said Dad firmly. "We have had quite enough interruption to our routine."

So Thomas stood in the hell zone that was gym. Miss Peach took no nonsense from her class. She had all the apparatus out in the school hall: the beam, the trampoline, the mats, the dreaded jumping horse.

All the class lined up ready to jump over the horse. It usually went with a good rhythm, that is until it came to Thomas's turn. Today would be no different, he thought miserably.

Thomas closed his eyes and started his run, waiting for the bump as he hit the horse, the shout that would be Miss Peach telling him he wasn't trying hard enough, and the laughter that would be his classmates.

Except he didn't hit the horse, and all
he heard was a loud gasp. When he
opened his eyes he was amazed to
find he was about six feet off
the ground.

Thomas landed
ungracefully on the
other side of the horse.

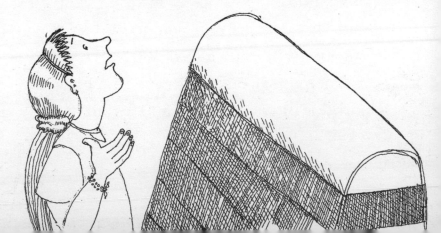

"Thomas Top, what do you think you're doing?" said a shocked Miss Peach.

"Nothing, miss," said Thomas, "just jumping."

The class was silent. Children can jump high, but six feet off the ground was unbelievable by anyone's standards. Miss Peach was seeing things, that was it. She clapped her hands. "Now everyone, settle down and let's do it one more time. Well done, Thomas, for getting over the horse."

It happened again. This time Thomas found himself about eight feet off the ground and heading for the other side of the school hall. He landed with a loud bump.

"That's it, Thomas Top. I will not have this kind of showing-off in my lesson," said Miss Peach. "You will go and sit outside until you calm down."

Thomas sat outside in the draughty corridor in his plimsolls and a flimsy white T-shirt and brown shorts.

"What are you doing out here, Thomas Top?" said Mr March the headmaster.

"I got sent out for showing off," said Thomas apologetically.

Mr March laughed. "Not like you, Top, you're always such a quiet little chap. Come on, let's see what all this is about."

The class were now on the trampoline.

"Sorry to interrupt you, Miss Peach, but this little fellow tells me he's been sent outside for showing off, is that right?"

"Yes," said Miss Peach flatly. "He was jumping too high."

Mr March looked puzzled. "Jumping too high? Well, I never would have thought he had it in him."

"Neither would I," said Miss Peach, who did not appreciate the headmaster's interruption one little bit.

"Well," said Mr March, "I'm sure Thomas will behave himself now, and perhaps he can join in on the trampoline."

Thomas had always hated the trampoline. He was no good at coordination; jumping up and down terrified the socks off him. He climbed up gingerly, his face pale.

"Don't forget to bend your knees," said Miss Peach sternly.

Thomas bent his knees and straightened up again, feeling very wobbly on his feet.

"He's not really trying, miss," said Suzi Morris.

"He didn't jump," said Joe Corry, another boy in his class. "He just bent his knees."

"Now come on," said Mr March. "I'm sure you can do better than that. Let's see you jumping nice and high."

What happened next gave Thomas the biggest shock of his life. He found himself going up and up towards the ceiling of the school hall, his legs and arms waving about before grabbing hold of a beam and hanging there.

Thomas was scared
of heights. They made
him feel sick. He was now
higher than he had ever
been in his life and he didn't
know how it had happened.

"Help, please!" cried Thomas.

"Oh my word," cried Mr
March. "Get a ladder, quick!
Hold on boy, we'll get you
down."

But it was too
late. Thomas felt his
fingers getting weak.
There was no
way he was
going to
survive this.

He was going to fall,
break both his legs, his
arms, his collarbone,
everything, of that he was
certain. He let out a small scream,
which seemed to be echoed by a
much louder one from everybody
down below.

He was falling like a stone. Thomas put
out his arms to break his fall and this had
the effect of making him go up again. This
couldn't be happening. He felt he was on
a rollercoaster. Perhaps it was all a
bad dream.

He would wake up in a minute and find himself safely back in bed with a nice safe sore throat.

Instead he found himself sitting on a beam high up in the school hall, looking down on his class and teacher who were all staring up at him, open-mouthed. He clung on for dear life while Mr March quickly ushered all the children out of the school hall.

"That's all fine and good," said Miss Peach to herself, "but the question is how are we going to get him down?"

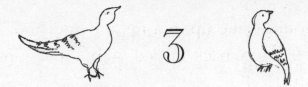

3

Mrs Top arrived at the school in a terrible state. "What kind of incident? Why have I been called here?" she said. "I have already had to take a week off work with Thomas being ill."

Mr March looked quite embarrassed.

Thomas felt miserable. It had taken over an hour to get him down. In the end Miss Peach had had to climb up and with a lot of gentle talking, which didn't come easy to her, she had managed to persuade a very shaky Thomas to make his way to the floor.

"Well," said Mr March, clearing his throat, "Thomas jumped."

"Isn't he supposed to jump, isn't that what they do in gym, jump?" said Mrs Top.

"Yes," said Mr March. "Not quite this kind of jumping though."

"I'm sorry, you've lost me," said Mrs Top, looking even more baffled.

The headmaster coughed. "Please sit down."

Mrs Top perched on the edge of her chair while the headmaster told her, using a lot of pauses and erms, what had happened in the school hall. He had to admit that it sounded rather far-fetched.

When Mrs Top had heard what the headmaster had to say, she stood up. "You have brought me all the way to school because Thomas jumped," she said.

"I am sorry, but I don't understand what you are talking about, Mr March. All I know is I should never have let him play games, after he's been so poorly."

"Thomas," said Mr March, "will you please jump."

Thomas looked at his mum.

"Do I have to?" he asked her.

"Yes, let's get this over with," said Mum wearily. "Then I can get back to work."

Thomas bent his knees and pretended to jump, keeping his feet fixed on the floor.

"There," said Mrs Top. "There's nothing wrong with that. He's never been all that good at sports."

"Thomas," said the headmaster firmly. "I would like you to do a proper jump, not a pretend one."

Thomas looked from his mum's face to Mr March and knew there was no way out. He closed his eyes and jumped.

He hit his head so hard on the ceiling

that a bit of plaster fell onto the carpet below. Thomas landed with a thud as Mrs Top fainted. She recovered to find the school nurse holding her hand and Mr March pouring a cup of sweet tea. Mrs Top felt flustered by all the attention and stood up, feeling weak.

"I think you should sit down until you get over the shock," said the nurse kindly.

"There is nothing to get over," said Mum, getting up and adjusting her coat. "We are just ordinary people and jumping very high doesn't run in the family."

"Quite so, Mrs Top," said the headmaster. "All the same, perhaps Thomas should spend a few more days at home until he is quite better."

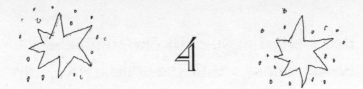

4

There was no way Mrs Top would be
going back to work today. She took
Thomas's hand and they left the school and
walked home. She looked pale and worried.

"We won't have to tell Dad, will we?"
said Thomas nervously.

"I am afraid we will," said Mrs Top. "He
would get to hear about it sooner or later."

Thomas knew this would be the worst
part. His dad prided himself on their being
just an ordinary family. They lived in a
three-bedroomed house that looked no
different from any of the other three-
bedroomed houses in their street. Mr Top
had a regular job as a button salesman, and
Mrs Top worked in an office. They were
ordinary people. Nothing extraordinary
ever happened to them and that was the
way Mr Top liked it. His dad would not be

too pleased to hear that his son had done something so out of the ordinary as jump as high as the ceiling.

That evening Mum told Dad what had happened at school. When Mum had finished Thomas gave a demonstration.

His dad smiled and said, "Rita my dear, boys don't jump to the top of school halls or hit their heads on kitchen ceilings. It is simply not possible for anybody to jump that high. I think this is a classic case of people letting their imaginations get the better of them." He laughed. "Perhaps, young man," he said, looking at Thomas's worried face, "April Fool's day has come late this year."

Thomas felt relieved. It wasn't exactly

what he thought his dad
would say. He had
imagined he was going to
be in big trouble.

"But Alan," said Mum,
"you must have seen him jump
just now. Thomas, do it again."

Thomas did as he was told.

"There you see," said Mum, "that
can't be normal."

"Rita, this is the last time I'll say it. Boys
don't jump that high," said Dad, beginning
to lose his temper. "I don't know what's
come over you, Rita. You will be giving
the boy all sorts of stupid ideas."

Thomas couldn't believe it. Surely his
dad could see him jumping up to the
ceiling? Mum was right, he shouldn't be
able to do that.

"I think," said Dad sternly, "that Thomas
just needs an early night. Then he will be
as right as rain."

There was a terrible silence, then Mum smiled weakly. There seemed little point in arguing. "Perhaps you're right," she said. "It is all a bit odd."

"Of course I'm right," said Dad. "I am always right. Now, we will hear no more on the subject. There's nothing wrong with Thomas. He is just an ordinary little boy. There's definitely no excuse for missing any more school. I will speak to Mr March tomorrow and put an end to all this nonsense."

Thomas sat in bed that evening thinking
fairies weren't fat, were they? All the fairies
he had ever seen in fairy books were thin
with beautiful long hair and wings that
twinkled. They weren't fat and they didn't
belch. It was hard to believe she was a real
fairy and if she was, had she the power to
make a wish come true? But then how did
the fairy know what his real wish would
be, or about Mum and the fairy cakes? He
lay in bed looking at the stars that shone
bright in the night sky, and thought about
all that had happened that day.

Suddenly Thomas felt as if a light bulb
had gone on in his head. He remembered
that he'd wished he could fly. He got out
of bed and gingerly stood on his duvet
cover. He wasn't quite sure what to do.
Then he thought back to the school hall;

he seemed to go up when he waved his arms and legs. That's it, thought Thomas, that's what had stopped him falling. This time he pretended he was swimming. He felt a bit silly doing a sort of hopeless breast stroke in the air. Except it wasn't silly at all. He was now way above the bed, flying around the room.

Thomas could feel the excitement from the tips of his toes to the top of his head. He felt it like a delicious feeling of melted chocolate. Thomas Top, nine years old, Thomas Top could fly.

6

The next day Mr Top took Thomas into school and spoke to the headmaster while Thomas waited in the corridor. Mr Top came out and so did Mr March. "Glad we were able to sort out that little misunderstanding," said Mr Top.

Mr March also seemed relieved. "Now I have had a night to sleep on it," he said, "I think you are right." He looked at Thomas. What were they all thinking of? Of course this boy couldn't jump that high, it was impossible! Really, this had all got out of hand. He was running a busy school, not a circus.

"We can safely put the whole incident down to an over-active imagination," said Mr March, "least said, soonest mended."

"Quite so," said Dad.

That was the end of it, as far as the

staff were concerned. His teacher Miss Peach, who had never allowed herself the luxury of imagination, was only too delighted to agree with the headmaster. It must have been the stresses and strains of teaching that made them think that such an unremarkable boy as Thomas Top could jump that high. Thomas hadn't done anything extraordinary. He never had and he never would. He was just your average child, nothing out of the ordinary.

Except his classmates didn't see it that way, and stories of Thomas's incredible jump quickly spread round the school.

At break that day Neil, the biggest boy in junior school and a bully to boot, came over to where Thomas and his friends were playing.

"What you got in your shoes then, Tommy Top?" said Neil.

"Nothing," said Thomas.

Shoes were a very sore point with Thomas. He would have loved to have trainers like everyone else in his class, but his dad insisted he wore sensible ordinary brown lace-ups.

"Nothing," said Thomas again.

Neil didn't look convinced. "Well, that's not what I heard. What I heard is you jumped and hit the roof of the school hall."

"Everybody just imagined it," said Thomas.

"I don't think so," said Neil. "Come on baby, Tommy Top, show us what you got."

Thomas paused. As no grown-up believed he could jump that high, he had nothing to lose by showing the school bully that he could not only jump but fly.

"Go on then," said Neil, "bet you can't, Tommy Top, bet you can't."

Thomas started doing his swimming strokes.

Neil burst out laughing and so did the other kids who had gathered around to see what was going on.

"Oh diddums," said Neil, "what are you…" He didn't finish what he was saying because Thomas was now flying upwards. He was a little bit wobbly. It felt strange not having any walls or ceilings to stop him from going higher, and also a lot more scary. Thomas was rather pleased when he came down and landed safely on the ground.

"Miss, miss," shouted a little girl who was standing next to Miss Peach, "look, Thomas Top is flying!"

"It must be fun to have an imagination and be able to see things that aren't there," said Miss Peach.

Neil was quite lost for words when Thomas landed.

"I would shut your mouth before you swallow a fly," said Thomas, smiling. It felt very good to see all his classmates look so amazed, as if he had just landed from the moon.

A near riot had broken out in the playground. It took Miss Peach quite some time to get the children into class.

"Now settle down, children," said Miss Peach. "I don't want to hear any more stories about jumping or flying. Will you open your maths books at page three."

After school finished the whole class had said they would like to come to Thomas's birthday when he had it. This in itself was quite something. Usually nobody wanted to come to Thomas's parties because of Mr Spoons the magician, who did the same old magic tricks year after year. But Dad wouldn't hear of having anybody else. "We've always had Mr Spoons since you were five years old. It wouldn't be your party without him."

It was not surprising that no one wanted to come, especially not when Suzi Morris had her party on or round the same day. Last year she had had Aunt Hat and her Magic Handbag, and she had become the most popular girl in the school overnight. Everyone wanted to go to Suzi's party. In the end she had only handed out invitations to those who had promised to bring the biggest and best presents. There had hardly been anyone at Thomas's party. But this year it was going to be different.

7

As the week went on Thomas's flying got
better and he became braver and bolder.
He even had the cheek to fly up on the
school playing field and get a football that
had been kicked high up in a tree, which
had gone down well with his mates and
unnoticed by his games teacher. So far no
grown-up had noticed him flying.

His most daring venture so far was to
go to the corner shop and get some bread
for Mum. Thomas had started walking.
Then he wondered, as nobody was about,
whether he could fly. It would be quicker
and he could test if he really was invisible
while flying. There was only one woman
out walking her dog and Thomas
wondered if she would let out a scream
when she saw him fly past. She didn't,
though the dog barked wildly. Oh well,

he thought, if no one can see me then I might go a little bit higher.

He flew right up to the top of a building and sat there seeing the world in quite a different way, watching the sunlight play over the rooftops. He was no longer afraid of heights.

Then Thomas realised to his alarm that he wasn't alone. Sitting a little way off was a man in paint overalls who was looking straight at him. Thomas felt a moment of panic. He only hoped that he was invisible to this man as he seemed to be to everyone else.

"The Fat Fairy, I take it," said the man. Thomas nodded, hardly believing what he was hearing.

"How did you know?"

"Oh, I know all about the Fat Fairy. I saw you flying round your garden the other day," said the man, with a huge smile on his face. "May I introduce myself?

I am Mr Vinnie, at your service."

"You can fly too," said Thomas in disbelief.

"How else do you think I got up here?" said Mr Vinnie, laughing at Thomas's surprised face. "Why did you think you were the only person who could fly?"

Thomas shrugged his shoulders. "I didn't think about it."

"What's your name, lad?" said Mr Vinnie kindly.

"Thomas Top," said Thomas.

"Nice to meet you," said Mr Vinnie. "When I was a whipper-snapper of your age the Fat Fairy gave me a birthday wish too, and like you I wished that I could fly.

I didn't know it at the time, but it was the best thing I ever could have wished for."

"It hasn't gone away, then," said Thomas.

Mr Vinnie laughed. "No it hasn't gone away," he said. "I have been flying nearly all my life."

"I didn't think it would last," said Thomas. "I was wondering if one day I would fall tumble to the ground."

"Isn't that funny. I remember thinking exactly the same thing when I was your age. Then I met other boys and girls who could fly and that was great fun. We grew up in the air, so to speak. We've all gone our different ways, but we still keep in touch."

"So there are others as well," said Thomas. He found this a very comforting thought, though he couldn't quite think why.

"Yes, scattered all over the place," said Mr Vinnie.

"And no one noticed you flying? Are you invisible like me?" asked Thomas.

Mr Vinnie's face creased with laughter. "You are not invisible, Thomas. Neither am I, though I am more invisible than you because I am old and people don't take any notice of us old wrinklies at the best of times, let alone when we fly," said Mr Vinnie. "No, Thomas, it's simple. Humans don't fly, so no one sees us." With that Mr

Vinnie flew up into the air and turned a somersault before neatly landing on top of a pigeon, who did not like having his feathers ruffled by such a large bird.

"Wow," said Thomas. "How did you do that?"

"I've been at this a long time," said Mr Vinnie. "Now show me what you can do, Thomas."

So Thomas did his swimming strokes.

Mr Vinnie watched. "It looks exhausting. Don't you get tired?"

"Yes," said Thomas, "but I don't know what else to do."

"You don't need to wave anything about. You just have to trust that you

can fly. A wish is a wish and it stays with you for ever," said Mr Vinnie.

Mr Vinnie showed him how he could fly without moving his arms or legs. It looked so beautiful, as if he had control over the wind and the air.

Up on the top of a building near the corner shop, while the sun was setting, Mr Vinnie told Thomas all he knew about flying. Thomas flew home in great excitement.

Mum was very cross. "Where have you been and what have you been doing and where is the bread?" she said.

"I'm sorry. I forgot it," said Thomas. He hadn't meant to. It was just the thrill of flying and meeting Mr Vinnie. It was no good saying all that to his mum. She wouldn't understand.

"Oh," said she, "head in the clouds, I suppose."

"Yes, Mum," said Thomas.

8

At first the magic of flying was so
wonderful it hadn't really mattered
tuppence that no grown-up was aware of
what an incredible thing he could do. In
fact it had been very useful. It had given
him a freedom which otherwise would
have made learning to fly impossible. As
he got better, he began to feel more sad
that his mum still couldn't see what he
could do. His dad had said nothing, even
when he had sat in the garden watching
Thomas do somersaults in the air. It felt
disappointing that neither his mum or dad
could see just how good he was.

As the evenings got lighter Mr Vinnie
and Thomas would meet in the park
where they could fly properly without
buildings to get in the way.

Mr Vinnie said that it was sad that so

many people walked with their heads
bowed down, looking out for dog poo, and
not seeing the magic that was all around
them. The more Thomas flew the more he
thought how wonderful everything was
and how being so high up with the birds
made you see the world in a different way.

Mr Vinnie told Thomas about his dad
and how when he was young he had
wanted him to get a proper job, like being
a banker. "But once you have flown up

where the sky is blue," said Mr Vinnie, "you couldn't be tied down to a desk imprisoned in four walls." So he had become a painter and decorator, which was just the ticket. He could work faster than anyone else in the business. Flying up and down meant there was no need for ladders and he could float on his back to paint ceilings.

Thomas found that he could talk to Mr Vinnie in a way that he had never been able to talk to his dad.

"Do you have any children?" Thomas asked Mr Vinnie as they sat one evening at the top of Alexandra Palace, watching the sun setting over London, turning it from red to gold.

"No," said Mr Vinnie sadly. "Annie, my dear wife, and me wanted kids but they didn't happen." Mr Vinnie smiled. "I am not complaining, Annie and me had a wonderful life together." He had often taken his wife flying. She couldn't fly, but Mr Vinnie was a strong man and, as he told Thomas, his wife was as light as a sparrow. Sadly she had died last year and Mr Vinnie said he thought he would never fly again. But then one day he had seen Thomas flying in his garden and he felt that he couldn't give up, not when there was so much magic in the world.

"I'm sorry," said Thomas.

"No need, Thomas, but thank you," said Mr Vinnie. "Annie would have been right chuffed to have met you."

9

It is hard to imagine your parents being young and when Thomas thought about his dad he couldn't see his dad as a child ever really laughing and enjoying himself. Dad was more interested in Thomas doing well in maths and things like that.

"There's no money to be made in having fun," said Dad. "To get a proper job you need maths." Maths, Dad told him, is the cornerstone of your future. But Thomas was no good at maths, whereas flying was something he could do perfectly. Dad, thought Thomas gloomily, could suck all the fun out of a day without trying. It was like their dreaded fishing trips.

Fishing was Dad's one little hobby. He bought every magazine and book on the subject. He prided himself on having the

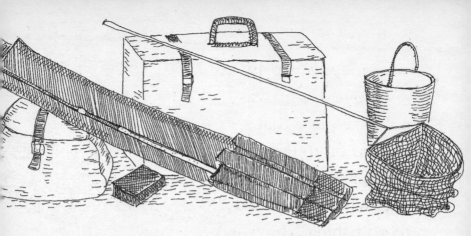

latest fishing rod and the most up-to-date
equipment. There was nothing Dad didn't
know about fishing except how to catch a
fish.

He would pack the car very carefully
on Saturday morning,
bright and early, making
sure nothing was left out.
It took ages and if Dad
couldn't find this or that
they would have to stop
everything until it was
found. By the time they set off
it was no longer bright, because Mum and
Dad would have had an argument, and it

was no longer early.

The reservoir was a dreary place that backed on to the local gasworks. This was where Dad liked to go fishing. They 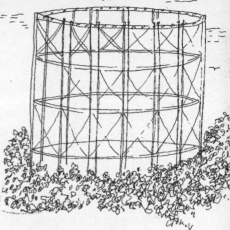 would arrive so late that all the good fishing spots would have gone. It hardly seemed worth all the effort, because in the end there wasn't that much time left to catch a fish. They would both come home tired and fed up and Thomas would wait for the awful words, "We'll get it right next time, son." His dad always said it and they never did.

There was no doubt that Dad worked hard. Except for Saturday's fishing trips he would spend the weekends studying his button sale figures. Mum would sit alone at the kitchen table looking through magazines and dreaming of what her house would look like if only she could paint it the way she wanted. Dad had painted it magnolia and brown when they first moved in. Nothing out of the ordinary, and that was the way he liked it.

A sadness now seemed to hang in the air like a mist. It had definitely got worse since Thomas had taken up flying. Dad had become more rigid, seeing less and less of what was around him. At times Thomas felt sorry that the Fat Fairy had been unable to give him his first wish that his dad could have fun. Then maybe everything would have been all right.

10

School was much better than it had ever been. Thomas had gone from being unnoticed, with only one friend, a boy called Spud, to being one of the most popular boys in the school. This was in no small measure helped by the fact that teachers couldn't or wouldn't see what Thomas could do. It gave him an edge over all the grown-ups, and a feeling of power which also frightened him.

His friends, like Spud, found it hard to believe that Miss Peach, who had seen Thomas jump and hit the beams in the gym, could not now see him fly. It seemed unfair to Thomas that his teachers would get cross with him for not being any good at games. For playing football as if he had four left feet while not seeing that he was amazing, a star. In the air, Thomas had a beauty and a grace that gravity had never given him. All he wanted was for just one grown-up to say, "Look, there's Thomas Top flying!"

Then one Thursday, not a very remarkable day, he had flown as usual in breaktime doing a round of the playground and few spectacular twists before going in with the others. Then he had sat in a very dreary lesson about Henry the Eighth, daydreaming about whose head he would chop off if he had been king. He looked at Miss Peach's dull face and her cold mouse-like eyes and thin lips. Yep, he thought to himself, she would be the first person to get the chop.

He was interrupted from his daydream by Miss Peach shouting at him.

"Thomas Top, are you listening? You are to go and see the headmaster immediately," said Miss Peach. She was reading a note that had been handed her by the school secretary.

"Why?" asked Thomas.

Miss Peach looked very red and blotchy. "Thomas, just do what you are told without talking back at me, and take your coat and rucksack with you," she said angrily.

This wasn't a good sign.

Sitting in the headmaster's office was his mum. She had been crying. Thomas felt he must have done something very bad, but he wasn't sure what.

"I'm sorry, Mrs Top," Mr March was saying, "but we can't cater for a child who is disruptive."

Thomas couldn't believe what he was hearing.

"I therefore think a suspension is the only course of action open to us, and we can review the case after the board of governors have had their meeting."

Mrs Top said nothing but took Thomas's hand and they walked home in complete silence. Thomas knew his dad would not be pleased. He would be grounded for weeks – maybe years. His party would be cancelled, he thought miserably and that would be a shame, especially when there were so many coming.

"It's not fair, Mum," said Thomas when they got home. "I didn't do anything wrong. I just flew round the playground and got balls out of trees, that sort of thing. I wasn't naughty or anything like that. And everybody liked it and now all my class want to come to my party and I won't be able to have it."

Mum sat at the kitchen table, her head in her hands.

"Mum," said Thomas, "all I want is for someone to see that I can fly and that I'm not making it up. I haven't been disruptive, whatever that means."

Mum looked out of the window at the birds flying past and said almost in a whisper, "I know, Thomas. I've seen you out there flying and in my heart I am so proud of you. But what could I say when your dad and all your teachers refuse to see it?"

Thomas put his arms round his mum's neck. "I'm sorry. I didn't mean to upset you."

"Oh, I know you didn't. It's not your fault, Thomas. What I would give to have wings like you and be able to fly!" said Mum.

"I don't have wings," said Thomas.

"I know," said Mum, "and you're right, you can do something so wonderful and magical that it fills me with envy. What is it like up there?"

"Pretty good, really good. People don't notice you. Only children and dogs stare. I have even flown up the High Street with my friend, Mr Vinnie," said Thomas proudly.

"Who is Mr Vinnie?" said Mum.

"He's a painter and decorator who has got his bus pass. He doesn't use it because like me he can fly. There are quite a few, Mr Vinnie says, but I have only met him. There's not so many children now because they don't wish for it any more."

"Why not?" said Mum.

"They wish for things like beauty and brains and long hair and to be the cleverest computer whizz in the world. It's getting rare, Mr Vinnie says, for children to wish for simple things like flying," said Thomas.

"I see," said Mum, who was seeing Thomas with new eyes. This was her son, her little baby, this incredible boy who knew all about flying! "Well, I think we should invite Mr Vinnie round for tea. I would very much like to meet him," said Mum, smiling. "Would you like to ring him and see if he can come next Tuesday?"

"But what about Dad?" said Thomas.

11

That night there was a terrible row in the house. Thomas had never seen his dad quite so cross. He wouldn't hear a word Mum had to say. "Are you mad, Rita?" he shouted. "Boys don't fly."

Thomas's party was cancelled.

Dad phoned up Mr Spoons, who said he was sorry to hear that, but pleased to know that boys these days did still get punished for being bad.

"He hasn't been bad," said Mum desperately, "he has only been flying."

"Will you put a sock in it once and for all with all this flying nonsense," yelled Dad, going blue in the face. "We are an ordinary family. Flying is for fairy tales."

"I can't take much more of this, Alan," sobbed Mum.

Thomas went to bed with tears running

down his face. He could hear Mum and dad in the kitchen shouting at one another, even when he pulled his duvet right up over his head.

The next morning things were not much better. Dad didn't say a word during breakfast and left for work still not speaking. Mum had to phone the office where she worked to say she wouldn't be coming in for a week, or until she could get some childcare sorted out. "I'm going to lose that job if I have to take any more time off," she said to the kitchen wall.

"I'm sorry," said Thomas, who had just come in and was standing behind her, tears pricking his eyes. Mum turned and smiled.

"It's not your fault. Come on, don't look so sad," she said. "It's just hard being grown-up. Sometimes we fail to see the magic in the world, and that's our problem, not yours."

Things didn't get any better over the weekend. Although it was sunny outside it felt like winter in the house. Dad was only speaking in yes's and no's. He went fishing by himself after making a dreadful fuss about a fishing hat that he couldn't find.

Mum had let Thomas have Spud over to play while Dad was out. They spent their time behind the back of the garden shed.

"What's in there?" Spud asked.

"I don't know. Dad doesn't let me go in. He says it's just for the lawnmower," said Thomas, kicking a stone.

The boys talked about Thomas's party and what a bad thing it was that it had been cancelled, especially when it had been the most talked-about party in the school for ages.

"Well," said Thomas, "in a way I'm quite pleased it's not happening. Can you see everybody sitting there and watching Mr Spoons' magic show for babies?"

"You would have to do a lot of flying to make up for that," said Spud.

On one thing they both agreed, the school was wrong to have suspended Thomas for just being amazing at flying.

"It's not on the National Curriculum, more's the pity," said Spud.

"Hey, wouldn't it be well wicked if Miss Peach had to give lessons in flying," said Thomas.

"I think," said Spud, "the teachers at our school are the living dead."

Thomas laughed. It felt good to be outside with your best mate and the sun shining. Thomas soared up in

the air and down again,
Spud running after him. It
looked as if Spud was chasing
a kite shaped like a boy. On
the last run round the garden
Spud hit the door of the
garden shed by mistake and
to his surprise it opened.
Thomas landed next to him
and they pushed the door
a little farther open.

"We shouldn't go in," said
Thomas. "Dad would
explode if he found
we'd been snooping."

"There's something behind the lawnmower," said Spud.

Thomas looked again, his eyes getting used to the gloom of the shed. Spud was right. Whatever it was was well hidden, with a large tarpaulin covering it.

"Go on," said Spud. "I'll keep a lookout."

Thomas hesitated in the doorway. But his curiosity got the better of him and he squeezed in carefully so as not to disturb anything. He lifted up the cover gingerly and looked underneath.

What Thomas was expecting he didn't really know, but he was amazed by what

he saw: a beautiful old motorbike with a sidecar, its chrome shining like star dust. It looked almost new. The boys stood open-mouthed, looking at it.

"Do you think your dad stole it?" asked Spud.

"No," said Thomas, "Dad would never do anything like that."

Still, he had to agree with Spud that it was a bit odd Dad having such a great motorbike hidden in the garden shed. They quickly put the covers back and made sure the bolt was properly fastened this time.

Mum brought them out some lemonade and biscuits, saying Spud should go home soon. The boys sat eating on the grass.

"A mystery," said Spud. "Perhaps your dad has another life that you don't know about."

Thomas didn't think so. He couldn't see his dad ever having that much fun.

12

It seemed to take forever for Tuesday to
come round. Why is it, wondered Thomas,
that the things you look forward to seem
to take so long, and then when they come,
seem to go so fast? But at last Mr Vinnie
arrived, looking very smart. He was
wearing an old flying jacket.

Mum had put the tea out in the garden
on a table laid with a white linen
tablecloth and a bunch of flowers. Thomas
had helped her make a cake. He had great
fun putting in the strawberry jam and
whipped cream. It looked a picture.

Mum and Mr Vinnie got on very well
and she asked him all the questions that
Thomas thought a non-flying grown-up
might ask. Like, is it safe? Will Thomas
hurt himself? Could the wind carry him
away? Should he only go flying when it's

sunny? Mr Vinnie ate the cake, which he said was delicious, and assured Mum that Thomas was doing very well and there was no need to worry.

"Would you like to see what flying is like, Rita?" said Mr Vinnie.

"You mean fly up there? It's not possible," said Mum, blushing.

"Oh yes it is Mum, it is. Tell her, Mr Vinnie, tell her," said Thomas in great excitement.

Mr Vinnie told her about Annie his
wife who was a non-flyer like herself, and
how they had flown together.

"You used to fly to France, didn't you,"
said Thomas, who now couldn't wait to
show his mum what it was like.

Mum stood in the middle of the garden.
Mr Vinnie took one hand and Thomas
held the other.

"What do I do now?" said Mum, feeling
rather foolish.

"Nothing at all, just hold on to us and don't let go."

No sooner had Mr Vinnie said this than Mum realised she was way up above the ground, looking down on the little gardens and houses that lay like a patchwork quilt beneath her.

"Oh, this is wonderful!" she cried. "Oh, this is magic!"

13

"What do you think you're doing, Rita?" shouted Dad as Mum landed back in the garden.

"Flying," said Mum proudly.

"And who is this man and what is he doing here?" said Dad. He did not look at all happy. Mum tried to explain and so did Thomas and Mr Vinnie. Dad was having none of it.

"I've had enough of this madness. What has come over you, Rita?"

It had ended very badly. Dad had shouted at Mr Vinnie, saying he had no right to come here invited or not, and

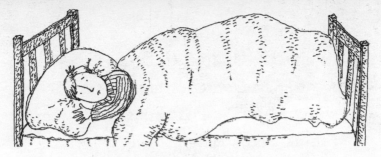

he was going to hold Mr Vinnie
personally responsible for all this flying
nonsense. Thomas was sent to bed early
and once again he could hear his parents
arguing downstairs.

The next morning he found Mum
sitting alone at the kitchen table. Her face
had a sad upside-down look about it. Dad
had already left for work.

"Why is Dad so cross?" Thomas asked
her as he was eating a bowl of Wheetos.
Mum looked out of the window and up at
the pale blue sky.

"I think it's Dad's work that makes him
so unhappy. He is most probably a bit like
you, bullied at work by his boss for not
getting the right amount of button sales."

"I'm not bullied any more," said Thomas.

"I know," said Mum. "It doesn't work being ordinary. Being ordinary is harder for some than being extraordinary."

"I think you are right," said Thomas.

Mum made a cup of tea and told Thomas what his dad had been like when she had first met him. He was so different from the other young men she knew, and that was what she loved about him. He was out of the ordinary. Like his motorbike, which had a sidecar and a name like a movie star – Harley Davidson.

"What happened to the motorbike, Mum?" asked Thomas. He didn't want to tell her he'd seen it.

"Oh, it's in the garden shed," said Mum. "But do you know, Thomas, your dad used to be a whizz at magic tricks? He could make flowers come out of his hat and coins from behind his ears."

"What happened?" said Thomas. "Why isn't he like that now?"

"Dad wanted so much for you. He was going to make our fortunes. We were all going to live in a grand house. Dad was going to be king of the button sales, except it didn't quite work out that way," said Mum sadly. "He thought he had to be grown-up and responsible, and he just got stuck. Time that goes so slowly for you just flew past for us. We lost our dreams. Anyway, Dad thought dreams were for kids."

Thomas thought, well, that explains the mystery of the motorbike. How odd, he thought, to own such a wonderful machine and keep it hidden in the garden shed. It was not all his dad had kept hidden, Thomas thought miserably.

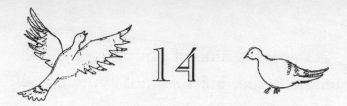

14

Thomas knew it was bad. His mum had gone to stay with her sister and she wasn't back. Today was Saturday, his dad's birthday, and he should have been having his party. He lay in bed wondering what was going to happen. He had made Dad a card and a little present, a painted box for his fish hooks. He was about to get out of bed and give them to him when the front doorbell rang and he heard a familiar voice. He got out of bed and ran downstairs in his dressing-gown, forgetting his slippers. His dad was standing in the doorway.

"I don't know what you want," he was saying. In front of him stood the Fat Fairy.

"It's quite simple, Mr Top. You are Alan Top, Thomas's dad?" said the Fat Fairy.

"Yes," said Dad.

"I am here to give you a wish."

"Is this some kind of practical joke?" said Dad. "Because if it is I am not in the mood."

"No," said the Fat Fairy.

"Dad," said Thomas, pulling at his sleeve.

"Thomas, not now," his dad said sharply. "Can't you see I have got some ridiculous salesperson selling something or other?"

"I am not selling anything," said the Fat Fairy. "Come on, do you want this wish or not? I am not standing here all day waiting. I have other places to go, other wishes to give."

"What do you mean, a wish?" said Dad.

"Oh dear. It is quite simple. You wish for something. When you've wished for it, I give it to you and I can be on my way," said the Fat Fairy, folding her arms firmly.

"I don't understand," said Dad. "Which company are you from? They should know better than to let you go walking round the streets looking like that, your wings all lopsided and your tiara that looks as if it's been sat on."

"Oh give me strength," said the Fat Fairy. "Have you any notion what I've been through to get here? It's amazing you were given these two wishes. Never known it to happen before in one household."

"Please, Dad, just wish," said Thomas.

"You were here for Thomas's birthday," said Dad, looking puzzled.

"Yes, I gave your son a wish. Now I am back to give you one," said the Fat Fairy.

"I don't need it," said Dad.

"Please, Dad," said Thomas again. He could see the Fat Fairy was on the point of leaving.

"Sorry, I can't hang around, dear," she said.

"Please, please Dad," said Thomas, who now felt quite desperate. "Wish to have fun."

"That's quite enough of this nonsense," said Dad. "Just pull yourself together, young man."

The Fat Fairy turned and started to walk away.

"You've ruined it," said Thomas angrily, "like you ruin everything." He was going back inside when he heard his dad say almost in a whisper, "I wish I could have... fun."

It was too late. The Fat Fairy was too far away to hear. Dad was still standing with the door open when suddenly the Fat Fairy turned round and looked at Dad. She gave a loud belch and said, "All this wishing plays havoc with my insides," and with that she was gone.

15

Dad closed the front door and started saying "You see, nothing has changed." Then he looked at Thomas as if he had never seen him before and started to laugh and laugh and laugh. Thomas looked at him, worried at first that something had gone really wrong. Then he realised that Dad wasn't laughing a hollow shallow laugh, but a laugh that comes when you are enjoying yourself.

"Oh Thomas, oh Thomas, did you see what I saw? The fattest fairy in the world. Well, it's made my day. Don't think I've laughed like that in ages."

"Yes, Dad," said Thomas, "it's your birthday treat. Happy Birthday!" He gave his dad a big hug.

"What did I do," said Dad, still smiling, "to have such a boy as you?"

Thomas went upstairs to get his card and present for Dad, and Dad went into the kitchen to make breakfast for them both. When he came down Dad was standing there looking at the wall.

"Awfully dull this room is. I never noticed it before," he said.

"Yes," said Thomas. "Mum wanted to paint it full of colour."

"I stopped her," Dad said sadly. "What a fool I've been. Is it too late?"

"No, Dad," said Thomas. He went over to the drawer where Mum kept her scrapbook full of all the paint samples and colours she would like to paint the house. Dad looked at it.

"We'll do it. We will paint it for her just as she wanted," said Dad. "Oh no, we can't! We wouldn't be able to do it in time. She would come back and find ladders up all over the place and that would upset her..."

"Dad," said Thomas, "my friend Mr Vinnie is a painter and decorator."

"I don't know about that. I think I was rather rude to Mr Vinnie," said Dad.

"It doesn't matter," said Thomas. "If I tell him that the Fat Fairy called he will understand."

"Why would he understand?" said Dad.

"Because he was granted a wish when he was my age and he wished to fly," said Thomas.

"Like you. All this time you've flown and like a fool I've pretended not to see. Life is just too dull and ordinary for that kind of magic. But now it's as if a mist has risen. My eyes have sparkles in them."

They had breakfast together.
Thomas gave Dad his card and the
little box he had painted which
Dad said was the best box he had
ever had. After breakfast, they
called Mr Vinnie who came round
straight away. In no time at all
Dad, Mr Vinnie, and Thomas had
got one room painted. With two
flying painters and Dad doing the
skirting, it didn't take long.

Dad and Thomas had one of
the best days they had ever had
together. In the evening they had
a takeaway sitting on the kitchen
floor, laughing and telling jokes.

Mr Vinnie asked Dad if he remembered any of his magic tricks. Dad did and said he had a few of them still locked in the garden shed. It was just beginning to get dark when they went out, and there along with the box of magic tricks was the covered motorbike. Thomas felt a bit guilty because he knew what it was.

"What's that, Dad?" he said, pointing to the tarpaulin. Dad pulled the cover off and there stood the Harley with its sidecar gleaming in the darkness.

"Well I never," said Mr Vinnie. "What a beauty!"

Dad smiled the broadest smile Thomas had ever seen.

"I used to take Rita out on it. We had a good time together. When Thomas was little we took him as well. We went to the seaside, we went all over the place..." He stopped. "I'd forgotten all the fun we used to have."

"It doesn't matter," said Mr Vinnie. "Why don't we see in the morning if this old thing works?"

"You could go and pick up Mum," said Thomas excitedly.

"Then me and my young flying helper will help finish the painting," said Mr Vinnie.

16

The next morning bright and early, Mr Vinnie turned up with a freshly baked loaf of bread which they ate in large slices, with melted butter. It tasted of white clouds. They filled the bike with petrol and to everyone's amazement it worked first time.

Mr Vinnie lent Dad his flying jacket and goggles. He looked great setting off on the bike, it made the most wonderful putt-putting noise.

Thomas and Mr Vinnie worked fast. They finished the sitting-room and Mum and Dad's bedroom. They laid the table the way Mum liked it with a white tablecloth and a bunch of flowers from

the garden. Mr Vinnie and Thomas felt
very pleased with themselves.

By the time Mum came back the whole
house shone and smelt of new paint. Mum
cried with joy.

"Oh my word! What have you done?"

Dad came in with Mum's suitcase.

"Do you like it?" he said.

Mum turned to look at him. "This was
your idea?" she said, amazed.

"Yes, I've been a fool, Rita. For too
many years I've wanted to be like
everybody else. I never saw what an
extraordinary family I have. Being like
everybody else means you don't exist. I
didn't leave it too late?" he said anxiously.

"No Alan, you haven't left it too late.
But what's happened to you?" said Mum.

"Well, I think maybe it's your birthday
present," said Dad.

Thomas looked a little baffled. As far as
he knew Mum had not given Dad a

birthday present.

"The Fat Fairy you sent me," said Dad. "She made me laugh so much."

Mum looked at Thomas and at Mr Vinnie and smiled. "What did you wish for?" she said.

"I wished to have fun," said Dad sheepishly.

"Oh Alan, oh Alan Top, I love you!" said Mum.

Dad was quite a different person after that. On Monday he and Mum went to see Mr March the headmaster, who agreed to take Thomas back as long as he kept the flying down. It didn't matter as much to Thomas that some people still refused to see what an amazing thing he could do. The most important people in his life knew, and that was all that mattered.

Dad rearranged Thomas's party and they didn't invite Mr Spoons. "He's jolly good with babies but not for you, my son," said Dad. Instead Mr Vinnie came over to help Thomas to give his friends a little go flying round the garden. Mum made a wonderful tea and Dad did some truly wicked magic tricks. It couldn't have been a greater success. When everybody had gone home Thomas stood in the

garden with Dad looking at the sun
setting.

"Next time Mr Vinnie comes round
we're going to take you up there," said
Thomas. Dad laughed. "Then I'll have to
cut down on the cream teas," he said,
giving Thomas a hug. "Go on with you.
I know you want to be off up there, but
don't be too long."

"Thanks, Dad," said Thomas.

18

Thomas flew to the park and sat at the
top of Alexandra Palace. It was his
favourite place up here with the birds. He
was thinking how wonderful it was to fly
when out of the blue the Fat Fairy landed
next to him.

"Hello, Thomas," said the Fat Fairy.

Thomas couldn't believe his luck. "How
great to see you again," he said.

"Just popped by to see how you're
doing," said the Fat Fairy. "I've been
watching this story unfold, dear. It tickled
my fancy."

"Do you know all my friends are
looking for you?" said Thomas.

"Everybody's looking out for me, dear,
but they don't often find me," said the Fat
Fairy, smiling.

"I want to thank you for making it all

all right," said Thomas.

"No need. I liked the wish you made about your dad having fun, it touched me, it really did," said the Fat Fairy. "But you can't wish for other people."

"Do you choose who to give wishes to?" asked Thomas.

"No that's not in my power. It's the Chief Fairy's decision and he's an old grouch. Always grumbling, and he doesn't have to do the leg work."

Thomas laughed.

"You should see him. Beats me why he should complain so much. He sleeps most of the time. All he has to do is give me a list of people and off I go. Out in all weathers, I am."

"Do you always go back and check on people?" said Thomas.

"Occasionally I have to go and remind someone what they wished for," said the Fat Fairy.

"Why?" said Thomas.

"Well, gone and forgotten, haven't they," said the Fat Fairy.

Thomas found it hard to believe anyone could forget a wish given by her.

"People grow up and they forget all sorts of things. Like your dad. It had got so bad with him that he had to wish for fun before it could happen."

"It was the best wish ever," said Thomas.

"I thought it would be," said the Fat Fairy.

Thomas looked at her lopsided wings and her tiara glinting in the evening sun, and said, just to make quite sure Mr Vinnie was right, "My wish won't leave me, will it?"

"Oh, bless your cotton socks. No dear, once you've wished for something, you've got it for life, whether you like it or not. That's why, Thomas, you've got to be careful what you wish for."

"I'm very happy with my wish, and so is Dad with his," said Thomas.

"You both should be. You wished for sensible things, things that could happen. Well, I can't sit here all day chatting to you. Must be on my way. Before I go I would like to wish you one thing, though," said the Fat Fairy.

"What's that?" said Thomas.

"I would like to wish you all the best, Thomas Top."